TH[illegible] SIL[illegible] WAVE

Best wishes,

BY

First published 16/12/24

ngkbooks.com

Check out other NGK books:

@ngkauthor

CHAPTER ONE

THE MURDER

The icy water rushed past the ship, black, like liquid death.

Their reflexes were sluggish, their body unprepared for the assault. The murderer knew they had one attempt at pushing their victim overboard to negate a struggle. With a violent shove, the victim felt their feet slip beneath them, their balance vanishing as quickly as their hopes of overpowering their opponent. Their body hit the railing with a sickening thud, the metal cold and unyielding against their spine. Water surged below, a maelstrom waiting with open jaws.

The body landed in the churning water, and their splash quickly disappeared into the darkness along the ship's side.

The murderer stood alone, watching the spot where their victim had disappeared.

No words were spoken; none were needed. The deed was done, and the sea would keep its secrets.

On the first night of its voyage, the Emerald Empress almost silently slid through the cold, open waters, leaving that dark memory behind.

ONE WEEK EARLIER
SATURDAY NIGHT
THE WINSLOW'S HOUSE

AT THE DINNER:
Lucy and Graham Winslow
Sarah and Peter Emerson
Denny and Terri Blackwood

As the last rays of the setting sun painted the Winslow's house in hues of amber and gold, two gleaming vehicles crawled up the short, winding driveway.

Lucy and Graham Winslow had lived in the home for a few short years, but it had never truly felt like home. The icy walls, creaky floors, and oppressive atmosphere whispered of a sadness that couldn't be explained. Their high hopes for this home and their marriage had never materialised. It was as if the house held onto past traumas, refusing to let go. Despite their efforts to make it a happy place, a lingering sense of unease followed them from room to room.

Adorned in their finery but not over the top, the guests stepped from their cars towards their hosts.

Graham Winslow, the epitome of sartorial elegance, stood on the marbled steps of his home, a welcome beacon to the arriving company.

His dark hair, slicked to the side, a study in precision, caught the fading light as he stood ready to greet each arrival. Inside, his wife Lucy put the final touches on the perfect table to welcome two couples for dinner. Peter and Sarah, Denny and Terri. Lucy's biggest concern for the evening wasn't the house or the food; it was people seeing the cracks in her marriage. Graham stood outside, rocking back and forth from his heel to his toes with his arms folded.

"He fucking loves it," Denny whispered to Terri as he stepped from their car, more slowly than they needed to.

"Get out of the car slowly," he told Terri. "They'll get out before us and take all the vomit-inducing Grahamness."

Terri laughed politely as Denny held her in the car, grabbing her between the shoulder and elbow.

Sarah and Peter Emerson had been a part of the group for as long as it had existed. To an outsider, they were a mismatched couple. Sarah was tall, had chestnut hair, and had a kind face.

She had always taken care of her appearance, especially when she knew she would see Lucy. The two had been kind-hearted competitors in every area. However, Sarah always knew that she couldn't match the cost of Lucy's designer clothes, expensive hair products, and makeup.

The only unknown to Graham was Terri, a fresh addition to the group, recently added as Denny's second wife.

"I can't believe he's only on two," he thought as he welcomed the first guests. Graham was always happy when Terri came along to a gathering.

"Something different for us to look at," Graham often said quietly to Peter, but Peter never knew how to respond. He disagreed with Graham saying it, but didn't have the confidence to call him out on his inappropriate comments towards Terri. Everyone knew that any attention Terri gave to Graham would not go down well with Denny, and Terri knew that, too.

"Ah, Peter! Marvellous to see you! That tie is quite the conversation starter," Graham chuckled, his words laced with genuine and practised deference. His laughter resembled a symphony that lured others into his world, where he paid meticulous attention to every detail.

Peter's tie was a mundane navy blue, unremarkable in every way, much like Peter himself, a good honest tie on a good honest person. Peter couldn't decipher if the comment from his friend was a subtle jab or a sincere compliment. It hung slightly crooked around his neck, a telltale sign of rushed dressing that evening. The fabric of his jacket was cheap and somewhat wrinkled, evidence of its frequent wear. As he smoothed it out nervously, Peter couldn't help but wonder why anyone would even bother commenting on such a lacklustre accessory. Peter was the nice guy in the group and rarely engaged in banter with Graham and Denny. Being honest with himself, he knew he wasn't as good-looking as the other two, had never been as good at banter, and had undoubtedly not kept as trim as them.

He straightened his clothes and ran a hand through his sandy-brown hair, now peppered with streaks of grey that seemed to have multiplied in recent weeks. The other two definitely died their grey hairs, but Peter preferred to allow time to take its hold.

He had never massively cared about his appearance and, in some ways, was proud of the slight belly that had formed on him in recent years. He felt slightly bad about himself only around Denny and Graham, their manicured hair and gym bodies.

Peter turned to his wife, Sarah, smiling with love and adoration for the woman beside him. Her warm smile radiated beauty and filled him with joy. Peter and Sarah, the group's steadfast couple, had been inseparable since college. They were an anchor for the group, a constant presence that brought comfort and familiarity to their friends. Their love was clear in how they looked at each other, their intertwined hands and whispered conversations.

It was a love that had grown and developed over years of shared experiences and adventures, solidifying them as a haven for each other.

Although Peter was safe, he probably compromised in excitement, and the other friends always knew that might be a problem for Sarah, but so far, it hadn't been. She had chosen safety over excitement.

Amidst the pleasantries and handshakes, Denny Blackwood's towering frame always cut through the crowd, his piercing blue gaze locking onto Graham's. As he approached, the air seemed to charge with an electric current, the joyful atmosphere giving way to an unspoken rivalry that demanded attention. Denny's blue eyes and dark hair looked perfect on their own, but they never looked right together, as if they belonged to different people. Denny's looks captivated people, allowing him ample opportunity to win them over.

"Evening, Graham," Denny intoned, his voice carrying the weight of authority while his eyes glinted with competitive fire, looking dismissively at Graham's house. "I see you've pulled out all the stops tonight. Your house looks so…cosy."

"Evening, Denny; good to have you." Graham held out his hand.

"Only the best for my guests," Graham said to the pair, the corner of his mouth twitching upwards in a forced smile.

"It's not every day we celebrate embarking on the journey of a lifetimc aboard the Emerald Empress." His voice got louder as he announced the ship's name, spreading his arms wide and smiling.

"Indeed, it's not," Denny said, still travelling away, his shadow mingling with Graham's on the stone beneath them. "And I must say, your connection to Edward Smythe is quite the ace up your sleeve. One might wonder how a simple food advisor managed such a feat, being so close to the owner of a cruise ship."

"Simple is hardly the word I'd use to describe my culinary contributions, Denny," Graham retorted sharply, "But then again, I wouldn't expect you to understand the nuances of fine dining."

Graham had been honing his skills as a restauranteur since leaving college, perfecting every dish and creating culinary masterpieces for years.

Edward Smythe, the owner of the luxurious cruise ship, the Emerald Empress, knew of Graham's reputation and asked him to design some menus for their guests. Graham felt eager to impress.

In his spacious kitchen with gleaming stainless-steel appliances, Graham handpicked the finest ingredients and crafted exquisite dishes that would tantalise taste buds and leave a lasting impression on even the most discerning palates. He poured his heart and soul into each creation, determined to make this dining experience that no one on board would ever forget.

The Emerald Empress would embark on a seven-night cruise around the Norwegian Fjords, setting off from Southampton and returning there a week later. As the main attraction of the cruise was the ship itself, it would take two full days at sea at the start and the finish, one day longer than usual.

Tonight's dinner party would be a prelude to the grand adventure that awaited them all - the ship owned by Graham's contact, Edward Smythe. All six dinner guests would go, and three couples would reconnect after so much time had passed.

Ever since they first crossed paths in school, Denny had been Graham's rival. The two constantly competed and challenged each other in sports or academics.

The desire to outdo each other and prove who was better fuelled their rivalry. It was a constant source of tension among their group of friends, but also a driving force for their individual growth and success.

Their constant competition, mainly during school sports days, floated beneath the surface, waiting for the right cue to burst forth.

The races they used to run, Denny's long legs and lean build propelling him towards the finish line, Graham's determination fuelled by the need to prove himself. Those days were distant, but the echoes of their rivalry still lingered. Their teachers sent them home from school many times when their rivalry turned into a physical fight. Both men secretly thought they could still take the other.

Denny, with his chin held high and an air of superiority, was never a popular choice. Yet, those around him always admired his unwavering confidence and self-assured demeanour.

A ripple of laughter escaped from Peter and Sarah, trying to be oblivious to the undercurrents swirling between Denny and Graham.

Yet despite the fun, there was no mistaking the steely edge in Graham—a clear signal that this was his domain, and he would not be beaten in his own front yard.

Graham told the other two couples that he had negotiated a significant discount on some of the most luxurious suites on board, treating his guests to a lavish experience they would never forget.

"You know he's giving us a 90% discount on our rooms?" boasted Graham.

"Why would he do that?" replied Denny. "What have you been doing for him in return?" he smirked and winked at Peter.

With grace bordering on defiance, Graham returned to his other guests, the perfect host resuming his role as if the exchange had been playful banter.

"Let's go inside everyone," Graham suggested.

Lucy Winslow, Graham's wife, glided through the kaleidoscope of the room, her slender fingers trailing along the edge of a silver-plated tray laden with canapes.

Each detail was a testament to her meticulous nature: crystal glasses catching the golden light, the peaceful symphony of soft music and laughter, the sweet bouquet of gardenias perfuming the air.

The luxury of the room was a portrait painted from Lucy's vision of perfection, yet behind her sapphire gaze, ripples of unease stirred. Lucy was a vision of calm and sophistication. She was beautiful and would always be conscious of comments from others that Graham was punching above his weight, and she quite liked that. Her blond hair, usually straight on a run-of-the-mill day, had tonight been curled, a sign of a special occasion, that, and red fingernails and lipstick.

"Everything looks amazing, Lucy," cooed Sarah Emerson as she walked into the room, her voice threading through the din like a delicate needle pulling at a frayed seam.

"With this level of organisation, it's hard to believe our little venture didn't take flight."

Lucy and Sarah had established an event-organising business years ago, but despite its success, they folded after just a few months.

Lucy's eyebrows shot up in surprise as she gasped at the speed with which Sarah had raised the issue. Her mind raced to keep up with her friend's quick thinking and assertiveness. It was a skill that Lucy admired, yet could never quite grasp for herself.

The words were honeyed, but landed like barbs on Lucy's skin. She turned, offering a brittle smile. "Some endeavours are simply stepping stones, Sarah. And look—" she gestured grandly, "—we've certainly risen above."

Sarah's eyes softened with an emotion that bordered on pity, a subtle acknowledgement of shared failures wrapped in the comfort of camaraderie. Yet something darker flickered there—a shadow of remembrance that neither woman could fully disguise and some things that weren't yet resolved.

"Indeed, we have," Sarah agreed, lifting her glass in a silent toast.

A chorus of voices cascaded around them, the banter of polite old friends weaving a tapestry of nostalgia tinged with tension. Denny's rich and resonant laugh carried across the room, and though it seemed to bring joy, it left a sour note lingering in the air that every single guest didn't like.

"Remember when Denny nearly capsized that rental boat in Majorca?" chuckled Peter, slapping his knee as if the memory tickled him anew.

"Only because you were too busy trying to impress Sarah to grab the oar," Denny said, his voice lilting with mischief. There was a collective snicker, a shared history that bound them all, except Terri, who laughed along and wasn't there but was conscious that Denny's ex-wife, Alice, was.

Lucy excused herself from the conversation, her role as hostess calling her back to orchestrate the evening's movements. With each step, she was the epitome of grace, her dress whispering along the glossy floor, her presence a soothing balm against the undercurrents of discord. She was calming to everyone, the kind of person you would be glad is around in any situation.

"Lucy, you truly have outdone yourself," Graham whispered, materialising beside her with a charm that felt both rehearsed and genuine. "Tonight is everything I hoped for." She smiled at him, but as soon as he looked away, her face dropped to something serious again, and she rolled her eyes. However, only after she was sure he couldn't see.

"Is it?" Lucy questioned, her voice barely louder than the clink of a fork against fine bone china. "Is it really, Graham?"

His smile faltered, just for a heartbeat, before he recovered. "Of course, my love. Tonight is only the beginning."

"You look amazing, by the way. Those Pilate sessions are starting to show," said Graham.

Their eyes locked, two seasoned actors on a stage. As the other guests raised their glasses, revelling in the illusion of unity.

CHAPTER TWO

SATURDAY NIGHT

ONE WEEK BEFORE THE CRUISE

THE WINSLOW'S HOUSE

The murmur of conversation swelled as the guests entered the beautifully decorated dining room. With his practised ease, Graham circled amongst them, a conductor orchestrating the prelude to a symphony of menace. All six diners were now seated around a large table.

The dining room was a vision of elegance and luxury, bathed in the warm glow of candlelight that danced off the sparkling crystal glasses and polished silverware.

The large, dark wood table at the centre was a masterpiece in itself, lovingly crafted and gleaming under the soft light. Plush velvet chairs surrounded it, each meticulously placed to ensure the perfect view of every guest.

The centrepiece was a lavish arrangement of fresh flowers, their sweet fragrance mingling with the aroma of the gourmet dishes.

As everyone settled into their seats, their expressions a mix of anticipation and curiosity, the tension in the room seemed to thicken like a heavy fog; they all knew that if this evening was going to go badly, it was here. Sarah's eyes flickered across the table, her gaze lingering on each person as if searching for hidden truths beneath their polite facades. Sarah's husband, Peter, watched her scanning the room with a suspicious eye, watching for every glance she made in Denny's direction.

"Well," said Graham, "Who would have thought it? Myself and Lucy are still together, and our evergreen couple, Peter and Sarah,"

"Peter makes it easy for me," replied Sarah, throwing him a wink. Denny took that comment as a jibe against him, the only one of the original six to get divorced.

"Wanker," he mouthed to his wife, Terri.

"Tell me you've all packed for the Emerald Empress," Graham announced, his voice carrying the vibrancy of a man on the cusp of adventure. "She sets sail in seven days, and I assure you, this cruise will be the talk of the season."

"What the fuck is he talking about? Season? What does that mean? Pretentious bastard." Denny whispered to his wife, Terri.

Terri remained stoic, her eyes avoiding contact with Denny. The tension between them was palpable. Denny could feel his heart racing as he waited for a response from Terri, wanting her to react to his words in precisely the right way.

Terri had always been a fiery and outspoken woman, unafraid to make her voice heard at any social gathering. But since marrying Denny, she had learned the art of silence and when to use it. His dominating presence had tamed her once boisterous spirit, and she found it easier to stay quiet in his shadow. No longer the life of the party, Terri now blended into the background like a muted painting on a wall. It was a small sacrifice for the sake of peace in their marriage. The group were all the same age, except Terri, ten years younger than them all, and it showed in how much of the conversation she could get involved in.

A ripple of excitement coursed through the room as if the very mention of the ship conjured the salty tang of sea air and the promise of adventure.

"Sarah is mentally packing!" called out Peter, always the vision of a traditional gentleman. His enthusiasm echoed by approving nods and dreamy expressions of the remote Norwegian ports that awaited them.

Each couple knew they were only going because it was an opportunity to have a holiday only millionaires could afford and their only chance to experience such a trip. Even then, going on holiday in this company, even for the experience, had been a close call for everyone. They wouldn't be going on holiday together through choice, and they all appreciated Graham's gesture of getting them all back together after everything that had happened.

Graham's smile never wavered, though a flicker of something indefinable sharpened his gaze for a heartbeat. "Edward and I are very similar. A mutual passion for fine dining, you see. He was rather insistent on my menu input," he explained.

A few years earlier, Edward Smythe, the owner of the luxurious cruise ship, had enlisted Graham's help to craft the ship's menus.

At the time, Graham was a small restaurateur who had jumped at the chance to secure such a lucrative contract.

Graham's menus had been revised a few times but were still being served on Edward's only ship, the Emerald Empress, the ship on which the group would take their trip. It was as if Edward enjoyed consulting with Graham and wanted to extend their working relationship as much as he could.

"Must be quite a friendship to have such influence with a man like Smythe," Terri added, the undercurrent of doubt threading through her words. Terri always felt like an outsider in this group, but tried to join in as much as possible.

Her husband, Denny, threw her a disapproving glance at the comment, as he always did.

"Yes, when you work on a project like this with someone like Edward, you get to know one another well," Graham countered smoothly, his tone a masterful blend of humility and pride.

Lucy just about managed to stifle a smirk, which Graham noticed.

"Besides, what are friends for if not to offer a helping hand when needed?" Graham continued, still staring at his wife.

"I also thought this would be a good opportunity for us all to put everything behind us."

Graham declared, expecting a flurry of approval, but his words were just met with silence, an awkward silence.

The conversation started to flow again around him, a river of words ebbing and swirling with the currents of curiosity and expectation.

As the evening waned, the allure of the impending journey on the Emerald Empress beckoned them all. Dinner had finished, and the guests mingled around, wondering how long they had to stay before leaving.

"Lucy, my dear," Graham said, turning to his wife with a glint of excitement, "just think of the stories we'll tell upon our return."

"Indeed," Lucy replied, her gaze lingering on the velvet drapes that framed the moonlit garden beyond. "Stories that we'll never forget,"

Graham's laughter resonated through the room as his eyes caught Denny's casual lean against the old-fashioned bar in the corner.

"Ah, Denny," Graham said, approaching with a glass of scotch, the golden liquid catching the light like amber fire. "I hope you've put those... wandering ways behind you for this cruise."

Denny's smile showed he was proud of such a challenge. "Old habits die hard, Graham. But who knows? The sea air might cleanse me of my sins."

Denny spread his arms wide in a gesture aimed at Graham. A few guests exchanged knowing glances; whispers fluttered like moths to the flame of gossip, but luckily, out of earshot for Terri.

"Let's just hope the only spirits we encounter are in our glasses," Graham quipped, though the joy was strained; the joke didn't quite make sense.

"Well, perhaps we'll finally bury the hatchet, eh?" Denny raised his glass, a toast to bygones that neither man believed would ever indeed be bygones.

Terri watched from across the room. Her confidence was long gone. She just wanted to get from day to day. Slowly, she sipped her non-alcoholic wine, the fizzy crimson liquid starkly contrasting with the ivory dress that formed around her perfect figure.

Lucy sidled up beside her, casting a sympathetic glance. "Quite the performance they're putting on," she murmured.

"Like peacocks strutting," Terri agreed softly, her voice tinged with resignation. "But it's all for show, isn't it?"

"Indeed," Lucy replied. "And speaking of shows, you must be thrilled about the cruise, Terri. A chance to see the world with such... colourful company." Lucy gestured to the entire room, always conscious that Terri was a newcomer to this group.

"Thrilled," Terri echoed, her tone flat. "Although I feel more at home amidst the pages of a book these days, than at these gatherings."

"You're not alone," Lucy confided. "Honestly, if it weren't for the promise of five-star luxury, I'd rather stay home with my cats."

A ripple of laughter passed between them, a fleeting bond amid the charade. But Terri's smile was short-lived. Her gaze returned to Denny, who was now regaling the group with tales of his latest business conquest.

"Thanks for being so understanding about the, you know," said Terri.

Lucy turned deadly serious.

"Never speak of it again."

Terri had only been married to Denny for three years, and her eyes showed a woman constantly regretting her decision.

"Sometimes, I wonder if we're all just passengers on Denny's ship, destined to crash upon his rocky shores," Terri mused aloud.

"Then you best learn to swim," Lucy replied, raising her glass in a silent salute before drifting back into the other conversations of the party.

Lucy always made an effort with Terri. Although they were very different people, Lucy always imagined joining such a well-established group would be challenging, but not quite as challenging as being married to Denny. Any woman willing to do that deserved all the respect they could get.

Denny had met Terri after his first marriage to Alice had broken up. Alice had been a complete part of the group until the divorce. The other four members had felt her loss and always secretly hoped they'd have kept her instead of Denny. Terri had been Denny's personal trainer during his mid-life crisis following his divorce.

They inevitably fell in love even though Terri was 10 years younger than Denny, and their age difference had indeed raised some eyebrows.

"Can't wait to see what Graham has whipped up for us on this cruise," Denny exclaimed smugly.

"Knowing him, it'll be decadent enough to make Bacchus blush," Peter quipped, looking around to see if anyone else understood his reference; they didn't.

Lucy watched from a distance; her lips curved in the practised smile of a hostess. The room swirled around her.

She had been drinking not to enjoy herself, she'd been drinking with one purpose: to get drunk.

"I'm sure, whatever happens, we'll have some adventures." Terri enthused, hoping some of the group's stories would eventually involve her.

The clock struck an ominous note, its chime a prelude to the unknown. Lucy felt a chill creep up her spine, uncomfortable in her own home.

Although she was happy that this evening had passed with no one falling out, so far, she knew there was little chance that the cruise would end without incident.

Peter and Terri stood by the fireplace. He studied her face, noticing the weariness that lurked behind her guarded green eyes.

"Terri, can I ask you something?" Peter ventured; his tone was gentle. "Is everything alright with you and Denny? I mean, is he...is he treating you okay?"

Terri's expression betrayed her. She averted her gaze, looking at the flickering flames in the hearth.

"We're fine, Peter. You know how it is, just the usual marital ups and downs."

Peter nodded slowly, unconvinced. He hesitated a moment before pressing on. "I just want you to know I'm here for you if you ever need someone to talk to.

I've known Denny a long time, longer than you have. There are things..."

"Thank you, Peter, but really, it's nothing I can't handle," Terri cut in, her words clipped. She forced a smile that didn't quite reach her eyes.

"Denny and I will work through it, like always."

Peter sighed inwardly, recognising Terri's dismissive tone. He couldn't shake the feeling that something was amiss, but he knew pushing the issue would only cause Terri to retreat.

"Alright, just remember my offer stands. Anytime you need an ear, I'm here," Peter said, placing a comforting hand on her shoulder.

Terri nodded, her shoulders stiff under his touch. "I appreciate it, Peter. But if you'll excuse me, I should probably check on Denny."

Peter watched her go, a knot of unease tightening in his gut. He liked Terri, but wasn't entirely sure it was for the right reasons.

"Terri," he said. Terri turned and looked him in the eyes. "I know what he is."

Terri turned away without saying anything.

Peter couldn't quite explain it, but his intuition told him something was brewing in the Blackwood marriage beneath the veneer of normalcy.

He feared that the fallout would be massive when it finally broke.

CHAPTER THREE

SATURDAY NIGHT
ONE WEEK BEFORE THE CRUISE
AFTER THE PARTY

As the last notes of a forgotten melody danced through the crisp autumn air and into the star-studded infinity above, Graham and Lucy watched their guests depart, their warm laughter becoming whispers on the wind. The house that had earlier echoed with forced laughter and clinking glasses now loomed ominously over them, its corridors waiting to swallow them whole into their shared silence. Cold as the stone facade of their home, Graham's hand hesitated on the brass doorknob while Lucy, her usually vibrant eyes dimmed by unspoken thoughts, stood rooted to the spot. Their smiles faded with the setting sun, replaced by an uneasy tension like an unfinished sentence. The distance between them seemed to stretch into miles as they turned to face the gaping mouth of their empty home.

Meanwhile, Peter navigated the streets leading home. Inside the cocoon of the moving car, Sarah's head lolled gently against the window, her chestnut waves casting dancing shadows in the passing streetlights.

“How was it seeing Denny?” Peter’s question pierced the silence.

“Peter, why bring up Denny now? After such a pleasant evening.” Her voice wavered slightly, betraying the veneer of composure she fought to maintain.

“Because,” Peter began, his grip tightening on the steering wheel, “we can’t just pretend he doesn't exist. Not when we're all about to be trapped on a cruise ship together. I want to make it okay, Sarah.”

Sarah’s face turned to a frown, the taste of aged wine lingering as she swallowed the truth along with it. She remembered the sharp sting of Denny’s words, the way they cut deeper than any knife could, but she buried those memories beneath layers of practised smiles.

“Darling, my relationship with him was a mistake—a momentary lapse, and it was a long time ago,” she whispered, her voice laced with the practised reassurance of a woman who had learned to hide her scars.

"It was twenty years ago. We weren't even married; we weren't even together."

"Exactly, a lapse," Peter echoed, the creases around his eyes deepening. He glanced over at Sarah, whose hands rested neatly in her lap, the tremor in her fingers the only sign of the storm raging within. "We've moved past it, haven't we? I really can't keep going through it."

"Absolutely," Sarah affirmed, a little too quickly and brightly. Her eyes flickered away, focusing on the blur of the cityscape racing by. The shadows seemed to reach for her, whispering secrets.

"Look at us," Peter said, breaking into a half-smile as he reached out and placed a reassuring hand over hers. "Stronger than ever. That's why I want to go on this cruise, to prove to ourselves that it's all behind us."

Sarah let the thought cross her mind that she had never met anyone as kind and loving as her husband.

"Stronger," she repeated, the word hollow as it bounced around the confines of her heart. She leaned into his touch, craving the warmth and certainty it provided.

Yet, as the car curved around another bend, hurtling them toward a future fraught with uncertainty, Sarah Emerson held her breath, concealing her fear from the man beside her who knew her best—and yet not at all.

The sleek sports car engine purred softly as Terri navigated the dimly lit lanes to their house, casting pools of yellow light onto the dark asphalt. The car's silence was thick, punctuated by the occasional swish of tyres over a puddle left from an earlier rain. Denny slumped in the passenger seat, his fingers drumming impatiently on his knee.

"Can't believe I let you talk me into this fucking cruise," he muttered under his breath, the words sharp as shards of glass.

Terri's grip tightened on the steering wheel, her knuckles whitening. She could feel the weight of his gaze like a physical force, disapproving and cold.

"You seemed to enjoy the idea at first," she replied, her voice steady despite the tremor that threatened to betray her.

"Enjoy? With all those fucking old idiots?" Denny scoffed, turning to look out the window. His reflection—a contorted silhouette of resentment. "I'll stick out like a sore thumb, thanks to you."

She swallowed hard, the metallic taste of fear tainting her tongue. "Maybe we could—" But the air snatched away her words as Denny cut her off with a mocking laugh.

"Maybe nothing, Terri. You and your naïve little dreams," he shook his head, disdain dripping from every syllable. "I should've known better than to marry someone so... inexperienced. Yet again, Denny was distracted by a pretty girl," he taunted himself.

The rest of the drive passed in a blur of silence and unspoken recriminations; Terri knew this had the possibility of being a long night.

CHAPTER FOUR

SATURDAY NIGHT
ONE WEEK BEFORE THE CRUISE
GETTING HOME

The walls of the empty house were veiled in shadows. Graham and Lucy stood amidst the remnants of the evening's gathering. Lucy watched as Graham meticulously straightened a crooked picture frame, his attention to detail bordering on obsessive.

“Bravo, Graham,” she said, the sarcasm in her voice sharp enough to draw blood.

“You managed to keep your fists to yourself tonight. Quite the gentleman.”

Graham turned, his eyes locking onto hers. A wry smile played at the corners of his mouth. “And you, my dear, played the part of the dutiful wife to perfection,” he retorted, the underlying bite in his words unmistakable.

Their eyes clashed, and they were two forces caught in a silent battle of wills.

They were chess pieces on a board where every move was calculated, and every gesture was laden with double meanings.

"Graham," Lucy whispered, a hint of steel in her soft voice, “I sometimes wonder what the point of it all is. We dance around each other like performers in a twisted ballet.”

“Because, Lucy, appearances must be maintained,” he answered, moving closer to her until he could smell the fragrance of her perfume. This scent once held promises, but now only served as a reminder of their mutual deception.

“Must they?” she asked, tilting her head to meet his gaze.

“Always,” he whispered, and vulnerability flickered in his eyes for a fleeting moment before it was quickly extinguished.

They were bound together, not by love, but by the intricate web of secrets and lies they had woven around themselves.

As they retired to their separate bedrooms, the spaces between them were filled with unspoken words and festering wounds that no time or pretence could heal. They lay in their respective beds, shrouded in the darkness of their thoughts, each a prisoner to the roles they played so well.

The night crept on, a witness to the silent screams and hollow dreams that haunted the Winslow's house.

Peter drove along the winding roads home. Inside the car, the atmosphere was warm, insulated from the chill of the night. Sarah watched the trees blur past, their skeletal branches clawing at the star-filled sky.

"Peter," she began, her voice laced with gratitude that made her chest swell.

"You've been... everything to me."

Peter glanced over, his eyes softening. "And you to me, Sarah. We've weathered storms, haven't we?" His hand found hers across the console, fingers entwining like roots.

"More than I ever anticipated," Sarah whispered, squeezing his hand, a silent thank you for not prying into the shadows she fought so hard to veil.

"Whatever it is," Peter said, sensing the unspoken words dancing on her lips, "we're in this together, always."

Sarah leaned back against the cloth seat, letting the silence wrap around them like a comforting blanket.

"Let's forget about Denny," whispered Peter. Sarah smiled and closed her eyes, aware that he had again mentioned his name. As soon as Peter knew she wasn't watching, his hand turned into a fist at his side, and the tension in his jaw was visible. He wanted to explode, and he wanted to live in a world where Denny didn't exist. The mention of Denny filled him with uncharacteristic rage all these years later.

Terri's car sliced through the same night.

"Why did you have to wear that dress tonight? Parading around, trying to outshine everyone. You're just taunting those two old birds." Denny's sneer was audible, and Terri flinched, feeling each word diminish her self-esteem.

"I thought you liked this dress?" she murmured, her eyes fixed on the road ahead, a futile attempt to hide the trembling of her chin.

"Like it? It screams desperation, Terri. Just like you," he spat, his disdain a tangible force in the confined space of the car.

Terri felt the sting of tears threatening to betray her, but she blinked them away fiercely. She was a porcelain doll, beautiful yet fragile, each crack meticulously hidden beneath layers of masks.

"Let's just get home," Terri said, her voice barely above a whisper, an echo of the strong woman she once was before Denny's cruel way had eroded her spirit. She didn't want Denny to know he'd broken her. She all too easily recognised the shape this evening was taking, and it didn't end well for her. It never did.

Peter and Sarah's car glided to a stop in the driveway of a modest house, the engine's purr fading into the quiet suburban night. Sarah, slightly flushed from the wine, leaned back against the seat, her laughter spilling out like warm honey. Sarah was beautiful, probably more attractive now, in her 40s, than she'd ever been.

"Home sweet home," Peter announced.

"Thank you for tonight," Sarah said, sincerity shining in her eyes. "For... everything."

"Always." His reply was a simple vow that wrapped around her heart like a comforting blanket.

They entered their home, the smallest of all their friends' homes, but a place imbued with the essence of their shared life—a collage of photographs, souvenirs, and memories painted in every corner. The familiar scent of vanilla and worn leather enveloped them, a balm to the world's chaos beyond their door.

"Let's not think about the cruise, just this moment," Sarah whispered, standing on tiptoes to plant a gentle kiss on Peter's cheek.

"Agreed." Peter's arms encircled her waist, pulling her close enough to feel the steady beat of his heart.

"Love you, Pete." Her words danced upon the air; light yet laden with the gravity of all they had weathered together.

"Love you more, Sar." He grinned, the lines of his eyes deepening in affectionate mirth.

The key turned in the lock with a forlorn click, echoing the hollowness that greeted Terri as she stepped into the dimly lit foyer of their large country house; each movement reflected off the cold, hard floor of the hallway. Denny's shadow loomed behind her like a nightmare, a silhouette of disdain that had long since replaced the doting husband. Without a word, he brushed past her, barging her out of the way, making her stumble on her shoes, his footsteps a march toward their bedroom.

"Goodnight, then," Terri murmured, a bit too loud.

"What did you say?" he shouted with caged anger.

"I just said goodnight," Terri replied, scared.

"Not so tough now?" Denny stood there.

"I'm sorry, I just meant goodnight."

This could have gone either way, but luckily for her, tonight's outcome was the best of all possible outcomes.

She watched the retreating back of the man who had become a stranger, her heart a knot of fear and hope twisted together—a paradox as confounding as the man himself.

"Fuck off, Terri," he mumbled as he went upstairs.

Denny paused at the threshold of the bedroom, the darkness within mirroring the tumultuous sea of emotions churning in his chest.

'What lies ahead?' Terri wondered, the balance of the potential downfalls of the cruise mingling with the anticipation of escape from the suffocating trappings of their lives.

Terri checked once more to see if Denny was in the bedroom and got out her phone.

Text Message:
I'm ok and I'm home, he's gone to bed. Thanks for the thing.

Terri pressed send on the text and quickly put her phone back in her handbag. She was exhausted by the evening's activities, and socialising with people she didn't know was exhausting, but keeping her guard with her husband was the most tiring thing she did every day. This was her favourite part of any day when Denny had gone to bed, and she knew there was a tiny chance of further incident.

This was when she knew she was safe and got to be alone. She often walked her garden at night. She had spent hours making everything perfect, the sanctuary from the world.

When Denny made her give up her personal training business, she poured all of her time into the garden.

Terri stepped out into the cool night air, the back door clicking shut behind her. She drew in a shaky breath and fought back the tears stinging in her eyes. Another argument with Denny, more hurtful words exchanged. This was becoming the norm. She couldn't remember a day that had finished without her crying alone.

She gazed out at the dark garden, the shapes of trees and shrubs barely visible in the moonlight.

Years ago, being in a cold, dark place would have scared her, but not now; anything that could happen in her garden at night couldn't be equal to how scared she felt in her own home. She now considered fearing things such as the dark, a luxury; people who were scared of the dark didn't know real fear. Feeling the weight of a full glass of wine in her hand, she took a slow sip, savouring the rich Cabernet. She hadn't been able to drink at the Winslow's party since she was driving. Now, she craved the numbing effects of the alcohol.

Walking further along the path, she let the tears slide down her cheeks.

Sobs wracked her slender frame as she gave into the grief and bitterness welling inside. How had her marriage come to this? They used to be so in love, so happy. Now, it felt like they were strangers living under the same roof.

Terri found herself drawn to the large pond at the far end of the property. She often came here to think and reflect. The still water, reflecting the stars in the darkness, was almost hypnotic.

Standing at the edge, she stared down at her moonlit reflection, distorted by the ripples from a gentle wind.

This was a safe place for Terri, but she couldn't remember Denny ever having been there. She drained the glass of wine in one, no longer enjoying it but knowing it was the quickest way to sleep for her. It was either get drunk or take sleeping tablets. But, at that moment, her eyes were taken by something she didn't recognise. She squinted into the darkness; something in the pond, or just above the pond, had caught her eye. As her eyes continued to adjust, the object became clearer, and Terri held her breath as, with every second, it looked more and more like the form of a person.

Suddenly, a shimmering form took shape, as if stepping through a fog, rising from the centre of the pond. Terri blinked, thinking it must have been a trick of the light and the effect of having just gulped down the wine. But the translucent figure became clearer - a ghostly woman hovering above the water. Only it's hollow eyes, fixed directly on Terri, remained clear.

This couldn't be real. Terri wanted to turn and run but couldn't, although she knew she should. There was a comforting feeling coming from the figure. She squeezed her eyes shut.

"It's just my imagination," she whispered. "When I open my eyes, it will be gone."

She opened her eyes, but the figure was now much closer. Its eyes were still fixed on her, looking into her. There were no secrets in it's eyes.

The figure started to move slowly and outstretched one of its arms, which now came into view in detail. An engagement ring and a wedding ring were on the same finger of it's left hand. The hand curled into a fist, extended its index finger, and curled it over and back, beckoning Terri to follow it. Every instinct screamed at Terri to run.

Terri took a step forward, being taken in by the figure. The cold and wet pond on her foot jolted her into motion. She spun around and sprinted back to the house as fast as her legs could carry her, panic rising in her throat. She didn't dare look back, terrified the figure would be right behind her.

Fingers trembling, she fumbled with the lock on the back door and flung herself inside, listening for footsteps following her against the jangling of the keys as she fumbled with them. She turned the deadbolt with a click and slumped against the door, her breath coming in ragged gasps. Looking into the garden, there was no sign of anyone.

"It wasn't real," she told herself firmly, even as a seed of doubt took root in her mind.

She poured another glass of red wine and gulped it down, it fighting its way down her throat as she still tried to catch her breath against it. She set the glass on the kitchen counter with a thump and headed for her bedroom.

All she wanted now was to burrow under the covers and shut out the world and the haunting vision that she feared would revisit her in her dreams.

She couldn't decide whether she'd rather be locked inside or locked outside with her haunting visions, which was a sad thought. Crawling into bed, fully clothed, she pulled the blanket tightly around her and squeezed her eyes shut, praying for a dreamless sleep.

Denny and Terri hadn't shared a bedroom for months. She knew they would need to on the cruise, and it made her feel sick. But Terri had got used to living day by day, and there were seven days until she needed to worry about how to handle it.

CHAPTER FIVE

7 DAYS LATER

SATURDAY AFTERNOON

SOUTHAMPTON DOCK

The sun dipped low in the sky, casting a golden glow on the bustling deck of the Emerald Empress as she prepared to embark on her luxurious journey.

The cruise ship exuded an air of sophistication and luxury, with its majestic decks lined with plush loungers and chic cabanas. Her deck was adorned with potted palms swaying gently in the coastal breeze, adding a touch of tropical elegance to the already exquisite setting, which may have seemed out of place on a cruise to the Norwegian Fjords but seemed to make sense in the evening sun of Southampton.

The Emerald Empress towered over the harbour, her sleek white hull glinting in the sunlight. The ship was adorned with gold accents and sparkling lights, giving off an air of luxury and extravagance.

It was the size of a small cruise ship, but seemed even more exquisite in its design and presence. Beautiful chandeliers hung in the grand atrium, casting warm, inviting light on the marble floors and intricate woodwork. It was like a luxury hotel that happened to be a boat. Plush velvet couches beckoned guests to sink into their soft embrace, while crystal vases filled with fresh flowers added a touch of colour and fragrance to the air.

The guests, dressed in their finest evening wear, moved gracefully about the deck, their laughter mingling with the soft strains of music that floated on the sea breeze. Sarah looked around in the car park and imagined everyone on board had taken the time to choose their 'boarding' outfit, as she most certainly had. The scent of fresh sea air mixed with the aroma of exotic spices from the ship's gourmet restaurants who served light snacks as the guests socialised.

A gentle murmur of excited chatter filled the air, blending with the distant sound of seagulls soaring overhead. The ship was a hive of activity, with crew members scurrying about in their crisp white uniforms, attending to every detail with precision.

A string quartet set up in a corner, their melodious tunes drifting through the air, adding to the ambience of sophistication and luxury. The music surrounded everyone and disappeared into the breeze. It was as if the ship affected everything around it, the centre of attraction in the port.

Just like the week before, Graham Winslow stood at the top of the gangway, waiting to greet his guests, a faint smile playing on his lips as he surveyed the grandeur of the Emerald Empress. Despite obviously not owning the ship, his demeanour exuded an unmistakable air of authority and ownership over the evening's events. He knew that none of the others would be there without him and intended to let them know. He spotted Lucy, who was arranging to hand the bags to one of the ship's porters. Guests of the Emerald Empress would leave their luggage in an office on the dock, where it would be checked in and taken to their rooms, even before they could get to the rooms themselves.

Lucy handed her bags to an older man in a faded blue cap. He wore the same uniform as everyone else, but the cap looked out of place, and it was apparent it had been worn for years.

Lucy imagined he was almost 70 but could look older than he was; the sea air had weathered his face. He smiled, the lines around his eyes crinkling. "You can leave your cases here with me. My name is Bill. Been working these docks longer than I care to remember; your case will be safe."

"Nice to meet you, Bill," Lucy said, returning his kind smile. As he hoisted her luggage, she noticed an anchor tattoo peeking from under his rolled-up sleeve.

Bill's expression suddenly turned serious. "Storm's brewing, miss. I can feel it in my bones. I always could. Some of the fishing boats I used to be on, they'd turn off their kit because I was so good at it. When you've been around as long as I have, you know when something bad is coming. I wouldn't even get on this ship if I was you."

Lucy laughed a polite laugh. She instinctively looked around to see if there was anyone to save her if Bill didn't stop talking.

There wasn't.

She couldn't shake the feeling that Bill meant more than just the weather when he said something bad was coming. Trying to lighten the mood, she said, "I bet you have lots of stories from your time on the ships."

Bill's eyes took on a faraway look tinged with sadness. "Aye, too many. Not enough good ones." Without warning, in a sad, slow voice almost under his breath, with a rhythm only available to a person of the sea, Bill started to chant:

"The sea keeps secrets dark and deep,
in graves where silent shadows sleep.
She hides her past in rolling waves,
and guards the lost in hidden caves."

Lucy, completely embarrassed, looked around for help, but there was still no one.

"I've seen the bones, the broken wood,
where sailors vanished, where they stood.
She takes her share without a sound
and buries all beneath the ground."

"Oh, that's lovely," Lucy said, hoping to bring an end to the recital.

"Still, every dawn, I cast my line
and watch her secrets twist and shine.
For though I know she'll not reveal,
I'll chase the truths she'll never feel."

"That was... uh.. lovely," Lucy managed, forcing a smile. "Thank you for sharing, but I really must be going. My husband is waiting."

Bill nodded, a knowing look in his eye. "Of course, miss. Don't go on this cruise."

Lucy wondered why Bill felt the need to stop her from going on the ship.

"Bill! We've talked about this. Stop scaring the passengers," called one of the other ship's crew, but with a flirty smile towards Lucy.

"It's fine; it's really fine; nice to meet you, Bill."

Lucy hurried away. She spotted Graham across the deck and approached him, trying to push down the sense of foreboding that Bill's words had stirred within her. Something was coming.

Lucy now stood by Graham's side; she exuded a quiet grace that complemented Graham's charismatic presence. Her elegant poise added a layer of refinement to their already sophisticated image as a power couple, despite them both knowing that their marriage was possibly past all points of no return. They had passed the Rubicon without a plan for the future.

As Sarah and Peter approached, Graham's smile widened, though Sarah couldn't shake off the unease creeping up her spine.

The way Graham's eyes lingered a moment too long on her made her skin crawl with a sensation she couldn't quite place. She exchanged pleasantries with Lucy, their smiles masking hidden tensions born from secrets buried deep within their shared past.

"Next stop, Stavanger!" said Graham, alluding to the first stop on their trip after a prolonged two-day cruise to Norway.

"I can't wait to get to the Fjords," replied Sarah, with a slightly disparaging tone about visiting Norway's third biggest city.

"Well, that's not the main attraction, this is!" Graham turned to gesture to the ship itself.

The four guests' eyes were drawn to a lone figure on the top level of the ship, an area that looked like it would be off-limits to passengers. A tall, grey-haired man looked back at them, too far away to gesture, too close to ignore.

"And there's our host, Edward." Graham turned back to the group. "I'm sure we'll get to talk to him later."

Denny and Terri approached the steps to take them on board. Denny was walking in front of Terri; the pair were not speaking.

"They've argued," Lucy whispered. "This is going to be fun."

Denny's charismatic facade barely concealed the underlying power play that always simmered beneath his interactions. Sarah observed the exchange, noting the subtle signs of dominance that Denny effortlessly wielded over those around him.

"Ah, there they are!" Graham exclaimed, his tone warm and welcoming. "Welcome aboard the Emerald Empress! I trust your voyage thus far has been pleasant?"

"You sound like such a prick, Graham," replied Denny angrily, his piercing blue eyes reflecting confidence and authority. Seeing the shock on Graham and Lucy's faces, he continued, "This ship is amazing. Edward Smythe has outdone himself." Denny was keen to emphasise that Graham didn't actually own the ship.

"He really has. I'm pleased to be friends with him," Graham said, managing a forced smile as he shook Denny's hand, each man trying to grip harder than the other. "Come, let us show you to your suites."

"What an ungrateful wanker," Graham said in Sarah's direction. She didn't even return a glance.

As the group of six made their way through the lavishly adorned corridors, they marvelled at the luxury surrounding them. Thick carpets lined the floors, and ornate lights illuminated their path from above. Even Denny gave an approving nod to Terri, who looked away, the argument in the car still circling in her mind.

"Goodness, this is extraordinary," Sarah whispered, exchanging glances with Lucy, who offered her a warm smile.

"Indeed," agreed Peter, his brow furrowing slightly. "I didn't expect such extravagance. What exactly did we do to deserve this? Edward must really like you, Graham." Peter wanted to counterbalance Denny's sarcastic comments. He was grateful to Graham for allowing them to go on this cruise. He knew Sarah would enjoy it, but there was no way he could afford a holiday like this.

"Ah, well," Graham began, a mischievous glint in his eye, "Edward owes me a favour from our deal. I thought it was high time he repaid it."

"Simply breath taking," Terri murmured, her green eyes wide with wonder.

"You deserve this, darling," said Denny, still aware that people could hear him, and he was still feeling guilty about the terrible week he'd put her through since the friends gathered for dinner and the car journey to the port. Terri had become practised at looking like she hadn't been crying.

"Edward certainly knows how to treat his guests," Lucy said, her voice gentle and measured.

"Shall we reconvene on deck for champagne and canapés at 9?" Graham suggested, eager to maintain his role as the gracious host. "We wouldn't want to miss the departure."

The guests had previously agreed to eat before they boarded or grab a quick snack on the first night, which took the pressure off them from socialising too much on the first evening. Since they had agreed on this a week ago, Terri had worried that Denny would be drinking and not eating much. Those nights didn't end well.

"Of course," Denny agreed, his tone suddenly sharp and cutting. "Lead the way, Winslow."

The group started their journey to their suites through the grand lobby of the ship, which was modern and luxurious, but not in a tacky way. Clean white lines, marble fixtures and beautiful down lighting showed the way.

"We should look for the signage to the suites," Graham proudly declared, acting as the group leader, a few steps ahead of everyone.

The lobby was busy, but the 'VIP ELEVATOR' was waiting for them. All six stepped inside the glass cube, edged with aluminium. As the doors closed, the bustle of the lobby disappeared, leaving them in silence.

"Ah, before I forget, we've already checked in for you," Graham handed Terri and Sarah their room key fobs. "Give it to the responsible ones," he said, to the inevitable eye roll from Denny.

The elevator rose above the lobby and passed an identical elevator going the other way, but with no one in it, passing them halfway.

"That's apparently why there is always one waiting for us at the bottom," said Graham, winking at Lucy. VIPs shouldn't have to wait for a lift, right, everyone? "A polite chuckle was barely audible.

"Right, here we all are!"

They all stepped out of the lift into a wide hallway lined with tall vases containing flowers. Clear entrances led to three suites, each with a vast space between them, showing their length.

"We're in this first one, Peter and Sarah in the next one, and Denny and Terri in the end one," declared Graham, again showing that he was making the decisions on this cruise.

As the other guests left to make themselves at home, Terri and Denny found themselves in the peaceful sanctuary of their suite.

The room exuded a sense of tranquillity, with soft candlelight casting a warm glow on the rich mahogany furniture and delicate silk draperies that billowed gently in the sea breeze. The suite had three rooms: a bedroom, a lounge area, and a bathroom.

"Who lights these bloody candles?" Denny laughed, removing his jacket and throwing it onto the back of a chair.

Terri sniggered back, momentarily annoyed that her smiling might have shown Denny that she was now ok about the argument in the car. Terri always remembered how funny he could be and just wished she could keep the good bits of Denny and not have the bad bits.

Denny approached Terri; his usual air of authority softened by a genuine look of remorse in his piercing blue eyes.

"Terri, I... I wanted to apologise," he began, his voice tinged with a rare vulnerability.

"My insecurities have blinded me to the hurt I am causing you. But you, with your unwavering patience and understanding, never give up on me. You know all too well about my inner demons, yet you continue to stand by my side through it all. And now, I can only hope you can find it in your heart to forgive me for my mistakes and shortcomings. Without you, my world would be a dark and lonely place."

At that moment, Denny stepped back to the chair and reached into the inner pocket of his suit jacket to pull out a small velvet box. Terri's breath caught in her throat as he opened it to reveal a stunning diamond ring that sparkled in the candlelight, casting prisms of colour across the room.

"I got this for you," Denny said softly, his voice laced with sincerity. "It's a token of my love and a promise to do better, to be better for you."

Terri's eyes welled with tears as she gazed at the beautiful ring, and a rush of emotions swirled inside her. All she wanted was for them to be okay again, for them both to be how they were initially.

She looked up at Denny, seeing a side of him she hadn't witnessed in a long time: vulnerability and genuine remorse.

"Denny," she whispered, her voice barely above a breath. "I... I don't know what to say."

Denny took her hand gently and slid the ring onto her finger, his touch tender and warm.

Terri gazed up at him, her green eyes reflecting emotions - hurt, love, and a flicker of hope. She reached out to touch his hand, feeling the warmth of his skin against hers.

"I have been a fool to let my pride and anger cloud my judgment. The thought of losing you, of losing us, it terrifies me more than anything else." Denny's voice wavered, a raw honesty breaking through his usual facade of control.

Terri knew she shouldn't get caught up in the moment, but amidst it all, there was a glimmer of happiness, a potential for healing and forgiveness.

Terri's thoughts swirled with curiosity as she contemplated asking Denny about his past relationships with Sarah and Lucy. She couldn't help but wonder if there had been something more between them; she didn't know for sure.

But she had always been suspicious. Although he had never explicitly denied it, he had also never been honest about it, and she knew it. But in that moment, surrounded by the peacefulness of the room and Denny's content smile, she decided to keep her question to herself. Despite their closeness, she knew Denny's mood was always fragile, and she wanted to protect his current mood at all costs.

CHAPTER SIX

SATURDAY NIGHT
THE EMERALD EMPRESS
NIGHT ONE OF THE CRUISE

The moon now cast an ethereal glow upon the deck of the Emerald Empress as the friends gathered around a high table laden with champagne and delicate canapés. A large flame, protected by a glass tube, raged before them, making their faces dance with orange light. Graham, ever the consummate host, ensured glasses were never empty while engaging in light-hearted banter, not pouring them himself but signalling to the countless waiting staff when someone in the group approached the bottom of their glass, which was not something anyone was used to, and it was hard to say no.

"Did you know," he began, his eyes fixed on Denny, "that this ship has one of the fastest engines ever built? I heard it could outpace any ship that does this route."

"Is that so?" Denny replied, his tone laced with scepticism. "And how would you know such a thing, Winslow?"

Peter, always the peacekeeper, stood back and watched as the two alpha males exchanged blows. His role in these situations was well established - to let them work out their aggression without getting involved. He had seen it all before, the posturing and dominance displayed between two men that wouldn't back down. But this time, something was different. Peter could feel his heart racing as he waited for the inevitable clash between these two dominant forces. He'd witnessed it many times. Sometimes, it would fade away into nothing, and occasionally, they would end up trying to kill each other. If Peter were a gambling man, this evening would be the latter.

"Ah, well," Graham replied, a sly smile playing at the corners of his mouth, "I have connections in the shipping industry. One must stay informed, after all."

Lucy also watched the exchange between her husband and Denny, her composed expression betraying nothing of her concern.

She caught Sarah's eye and shared a knowing glance that spoke volumes.

Sarah gestured to Lucy to join her in looking out at the sea, only a few steps away.
"I just can't bear these two doing this," said Sarah.
"I know, honestly, I love Graham, but this is the least attractive I ever find him when he's doing this with Denny. It's never going to change. It's been the same since college," said Lucy.
"I assume he still doesn't know about you and Denny? Back in the day?" Said Sarah, avoiding eye contact.
Lucy sighed. "I'd love to tell him, Sar, but it would kill him almost as much as the secret kills me."
Still looking out to sea, Sarah put her arm on her friend's shoulder. "Lucy, you're not just hiding a relationship; he was horrible to you, with the…"
"I know," Lucy cut her off. "I didn't want to be anywhere near him, but Graham was so keen on this cruise, so I just went along with it," said Lucy.
"Well, Peter knows about me and Denny, and I sometimes wish he didn't," said Sarah.
"Really? Everything?" said Lucy.
"He's such a kind, amazing man, Luce; I still feel horrible 20 years later.
He doesn't know everything, but that's for the best." Sarah returned to face the party, signalling they should re-join the group.

"The worst thing of all was that we let Denny get between us," Lucy said with a resignation.

"I'm sorry."

"Me too."

The pair exchanged a genuine look; everything was behind them, and now they were pure friends.

"Peter is just so calm all the time," said Sarah. "I just don't know how he'd react if I told him how Denny treated me; he's one of those people that just bottles it up, then now and then, just bubbles over. I think the whole time I've known him since college, he's lost it once or twice, but when he does, he does; something comes over him."

"At you?" said Lucy.

"No, never," Sarah shook her head, almost disgusted at the suggestion. "Always defending me, which is why he can't know what happened with Denny. I don't know what he'd do."

Simultaneously, their gazes shifted to Terri, the woman currently in danger, who stood solemnly by Denny's side.

Her expression was blank, and her eyes seemed to hold a depth of emptiness as she remained completely still, almost like a statue carved from stone. Not even the slightest hint of emotion played across her face. Sarah and Lucy knew this look only too well.

A familiar loud buzz of adults who had been drinking for a few hours filled the deck.

The air was full with a palpable sense of magic and excitement. The once quiet outside deck had come alive, bustling with activity as more passengers filled the space. The string quartet now graced the deck with their melodic tunes, their instruments gleaming in the moonlight. Every note they played added to the enchanting atmosphere, drawing on even more curious onlookers. Each of the passengers knew they would never forget that night. It was like a spell had been cast upon the ship, captivating everyone in its grasp.

This is the point in the evening when they first noticed the storm. A distant crack of thunder stopped the group in their tracks, and they paused mid-conversation. Dark clouds roiled ominously in the distance, swirling like smoke signals of impending trouble.

The wind picked up, rustling their clothes and carrying the scent of rain with it. “Look there,” Lucy pointed, eyes wide with realisation as they watched the storm approach, its jagged edges framed by lightning flashes illuminating the darkening sky. A chill ran through them as they understood: they were headed straight into it.

Graham stood apart from the others, his eyes fixed intently on the ship's owner, Edward Smythe. Although he hadn’t yet made it to the group, he was circulating among the passengers. Graham wanted this interaction to go well, in front of Denny and his wife, Lucy.

As Edward approached, the group instinctively parted to make way for him. Their conversations died to murmurs as they waited for Edward's attention.

“Good evening, everyone,” Edward said with a warm smile, his deep voice carrying across the deck. “I hope you're all enjoying your cruise so far.” Although he was much older than everyone in the group, Edward had charisma like no one had ever experienced.

The group responded with polite nods and murmurs of agreement before Edward's gaze settled on Graham.

"Graham, it's been a while since we've last seen each other."

Graham swallowed hard, feeling a lump form in his throat as he replied, "Yes, it has been too long."

"I've been monitoring your career," Edward continued, his tone still friendly but with a hint of something else underneath. "You've done well for yourself. I hope creating the menus for my humble ship has helped?"

Graham felt relief flood through him at those words before realising that Edward was waiting for an answer.

"Thank you," he said.

Edward nodded in acknowledgement before turning to face Denny. "And Mr. Blackwood, Graham has told me so much about you." Denny knew Edward was being polite, as the pair had just said they hadn't spoken for a while.

However, Denny beamed at the recognition of such an influential figure. "Thank you, Mr. Smythe."

Edward gave a slight nod before turning to Lucy and Sarah. "And how are you two lovely ladies enjoying the cruise?"

"We're having a wonderful time," Lucy replied with a genuine smile.

"That's what I like to hear," Edward said with a wink.

"Thanks again for having us!" Graham blurted out to Edward as he walked away.

Edward turned, and his gaze swept over the group, assessing each person with a keen eye before settling back on Graham. "The pleasure is mine, Mr. Winslow. It's an honour to have you on the Emerald Empress."

Graham looked relieved at the warmness of Edward's welcome.

"It's always a pleasure to host esteemed guests such as yourselves."

"Thank you," Graham replied, raising his glass halfway. "This is going to be a wonderful trip."

"Of course," Edward agreed, his eyes narrowing ever so slightly. "Well, enjoy your time aboard, everyone."

As Edward turned to leave, Graham observed his eyes lingered on Lucy and Sarah for longer than would go unnoticed.

Denny, who had been watching the exchange between Graham and Edward, couldn't help but stroll over with a smug grin playing on his face. He sidled up to Graham, his tall frame casting a shadow over the very conversation.

"Well, well, Graham," Denny drawled, his voice smooth like velvet but with a sharp edge that sliced through the air. "It seems our host didn't seem too pleased to see you. Could your reputation finally have caught up with you, old friend?"

Graham's facade faltered briefly before he regained his composure, a forced chuckle escaping his lips. "Oh, Denny, you always have a way with words." He shot back with a sarcastic smile, trying to mask the unease in his eyes.

Champagne turned into cocktails.

The storm loomed closer now, dark and menacing. Their once-distant hope that it might pass them by was shattered; they barrelled headfirst toward it. The sky grew darker with each passing moment, and the winds increased in intensity. Jagged lightning bolts streaked across the sky, illuminating the looming clouds and the ocean with an eerie glow. Thunder rumbled in the distance, growing louder and more frequent as they drew nearer to the heart of the storm.

Sensing the shift in the atmosphere, the passengers gathered closer on deck, wrapping soft blankets over their shoulders as they exchanged cautious glances.

Sarah's warm presence seemed to anchor them amidst the rising tension. Lucy, her gaze flitting between Graham and Denny, reached for a cocktail glass, her fingers trembling imperceptibly.

"We should never have come on this cruise," Sarah said, looking forward into the distance.

Terri turned to Sarah, her expression a mix of vulnerability and gratitude. "Sarah, I don't know what I would do without you and Lucy on this trip. This whole situation with Denny... it's unravelling me."

Sarah's smile was soft yet resolute. "You don't have to face this alone, Terri. You have us by your side, always. We will protect you from whatever storm may come, just like we've always done for each other. You may be much younger than us, but women care for women."

Lucy, unable to contain her turmoil any longer, interjected, with a tremor in her voice, "Sarah's right, Terri. We are here for you through thick and thin."

A sudden burst of laughter echoed across the deck, drawing Graham's attention as he watched Denny charm a group of fellow passengers effortlessly.

He could feel the muscles in his jaw tightening, and his eyes narrowed with each charismatic word Denny spoke.

“Still quite the charmer, isn't he?” Peter observed, following Graham's gaze and noting the subtle resentment etched upon his features.

“Indeed,” Graham replied tersely, barely suppressing a sneer as he took a long sip of his wine. His mind raced with thoughts of how to regain the upper hand, to assert his dominance over his so-called friend, his biggest rival.

“I’m amazed you’re not ready to kill him, Peter,” said Graham.

“What do you mean?” Peter already knew.

“Um, you know, Sarah, what happened with Sarah? I’m just surprised you’re ok with him.”

“Well, it wouldn’t solve anything,” said Peter, wishing he could actually do something about it.

Terri approached the pair, cutting the conversation short.

“Would you like me to fetch him, Graham?” Terri offered; her voice was laced with concern as she noticed the escalating unease among their party.

“No, no,” Graham insisted, forcing a tight smile onto his face. “Let him enjoy his moment.”

The others exchanged uneasy glances as they continued picking at their extravagant snacks, now served at their cocktail table on the deck, the cold air being heated by one patio heater per person. The group noticed that the wind picking up had blown out some of the candles on deck and was blowing around loose napkins. Sarah attempted to steer the conversation towards lighter fare, but the effort felt strained and false.

"Did you hear about the new exhibit opening at the Metropolitan Museum next month?" she asked, trying to mask her discomfort.

"Ah, yes," Lucy said, grateful for the distraction. "I've been looking forward to it for quite some time." But even as she spoke, she couldn't help but steal glances at her husband, her heart constricting with anxiety as she observed his growing jealousy.

Graham stood abruptly from the table, unable to contain his frustration any longer.

"Excuse me," he muttered, his voice tight with suppressed anger. As he strode towards Denny, the others exchanged worried looks, sensing the imminent collision of egos and the potential fallout.

"Having a good time, Denny?" Graham asked through gritted teeth, his eyes fixed on the man who had become both an object of envy and disdain in his mind.

"Ah, Graham!" Denny exclaimed, feigning surprise. "Just making some new acquaintances, nothing more."

"Of course," Graham replied, his tone dripping with sarcasm. "But perhaps you should remember who you're here with, hmm? Our food is here."

Denny made no effort to move.

"Enjoy your evening, Denny," Graham managed to say, forcing a smile as he turned on his heel and walked away, his heart pounding with rage and unease.

"I'm coming with you," Denny replied.

The low hum of the Emerald Empress's engines echoed through the night. Having decided it was getting too cold outside, the friends moved cautiously through the ship back towards their rooms. The distant sound of dwindling laughter echoed behind them. They were like elegant marionettes dancing on a gilded stage, their strings pulled by an invisible hand.

With each glance over her shoulder, Lucy couldn't help but notice Edward Smythe lingering nearby. It seemed as though no matter where she turned, he was always watching and observing with a curious intensity. A sense of unease settled in Lucy's stomach as she wondered what was driving his constant surveillance of the group. Was he simply curious, or was there something darker at play?

CHAPTER SEVEN

SATURDAY NIGHT

THE EMERALD EMPRESS

NIGHT ONE OF THE CRUISE

As the guests started to move towards their rooms, the once serene waters began to churn and swell, tossing the Emerald Empress back and forth, noticeable to even the most seaworthy of passengers. The passengers stumbled back to their cabins, clutching onto railings for support as the winds howled in their ears, a fierce reminder of the unpredictable power of the sea.

The murmur of contented goodbyes echoed around them, wrapped in their satisfaction, and trickled into the dimly lit corridors. The evening, an elaborate affair with a decadent spread and effervescent laughter, seemed to have succeeded in the way that no one had fallen out in the group, no fights at all.

"Goodnight, Peter," Denny's voice boomed, his hand clapping the man's back with more force than necessary.

"And Graham, try not to mope so much. It's unbecoming."

"Goodnight, Denny," he muttered, exchanging wary glances as they shuffled away from his imposing figure.

Denny turned and focused on Terri, who was hovering by the doorway.

"Terri, in now," he commanded, the charm of the evening slipping away like a discarded mask.

In their suite, the tension carefully tucked away during dinner bubbled to the surface. Terri's heart raced, and the walls closed on her as Denny's figure loomed large.

"Another splendid evening ruined by your sullen mood," Denny spat, the alcohol taking away his earlier kindness.

"I was not sullen, Denny; I was just tired," Terri replied, her voice barely above a whisper, her words measured and cautious.

"Ha!" Denny scoffed. "Tired, or perhaps ashamed? Ashamed that you're nothing but a bland little sparrow among peacocks?"

"Denny, please," she pleaded, her green eyes searching for a hint of the man she once knew, knowing he was trying to start a fight. The cruelty in his gaze held no trace of tenderness.

"I'm so grateful for the ring you got me. We said we'd try to be nice to each other on this trip."

"Enough," he sneered, his back turning on her as he paced the room. "I won't spend another minute suffocating in this mockery of a marriage. I'm going for a walk." Denny threw his arms around like a drunk person does. It was clear to Terri just how drunk he was.

"Alone? Now?" Terri's concern was palpable, her words tinged with fear. "There's a storm brewing. It's not safe. Stay here."

"I'd rather take my chances up there than spend one more minute looking at you. A personal trainer that gets involved with her clients. I know I wouldn't have been the first, and I won't be the last." Denny barked.

"Don't be cruel, Denny," Terri said as she sat at the end of the bed and started to cry.

Denny, more drunk than he was letting on, struggled to put his shoes back on.

"Since when do you care about my safety?" he retorted, his laugh hollow. "Besides, a bit of rain never hurt anyone. I need fresh air... away from you." Denny pulled on a waterproof coat that he still had from his years of climbing in the Alps.

"And don't worry, if I get struck by lightning, you'll enjoy the pay-out you get that I worked so hard for and you did fuck all for."

"Denny, don't go," Terri pleaded.

"You don't get to tell me what to do; good luck, Terri. I hope everything works out for you."

With that, Denny stormed out, slamming the door behind him. He left Terri alone in the luxury, which felt colder than ever. She sank onto the edge of the bed, the weight of years of unhappiness pressing down on her. She would get off the ship instantly if she could, but she was trapped.

Down the hall, behind another closed door, Sarah watched Peter take off his jacket. She knew this wasn't the right time to mention Denny, but she couldn't help herself.

"Peter," Sarah began, her voice trembling as she faced her husband, "there's something I've never told you about Denny and me."

Sitting on the edge of their bed, Peter looked up, his concern etched across his face. He knew he didn't want to hear whatever it was. "What is it, Sarah? You can tell me anything."

She sighed; a sound laden with regret.

"It was before I met you," she started, gathering her strength. "Denny and I were involved, which you already know, but it wasn't good. He hurt me, not just emotionally. I thought I could leave it all behind when I married you, but seeing him again—it's just brought it back to me like I was there again."

Peter looked like the bottom had fallen through his world, and Sarah saw something in his eyes that she had hardly ever seen: rage.

"Fuck Sarah," Peter said, reaching for her hand. "Why didn't you say something sooner?"

"Because I thought it was over, that I'd moved on. I thought I'd put it behind me." Sarah's eyes glistened with tears.

"But I realise now it's not just my past at stake. Terri, she's in danger. I need to protect her. I know what he's capable of."

"Terri?" Peter's brow furrowed. "What do you mean?"

"Never mind," she cut off abruptly, shaking her head. "Just know that I despise that man, and if he's up to his old tricks with Terri..."

"Say no more," Peter assured her, his voice firm with resolve.

"We'll protect Terri together. I won't let anyone hurt you or her."

"Thank you," As the weight of confession left her, the couple held onto each other.

"Thank you for telling me, Sarah," Peter said. Sarah could tell he was tensing every muscle in his body. The rage that she'd only seen a few times was there again.

In the other suite, Graham's hand slammed against the wall, a sharp retort to the silence that had settled between them since they had returned to the room. Lucy flinched, her back pressed to the cold plaster as if she could escape into it.

"Every time he enters the room, you're all eyes for him," Graham spat, his words laced with venom. "Do you think I don't notice?"

"Stop it, Graham," Lucy's voice was steady, but her eyes betrayed the fear simmering beneath the surface. "This isn't about Denny. This is about us, about you not trusting me."

"Trust?" He laughed, a harsh sound that echoed mockingly in the small space.

"How can I trust you when every whisper, every laugh shared with him, slices through me like a knife?"

"You're being ridiculous." She tried to push past him, but he blocked her way, his lean frame rigid with anger.

"Am I?" His dark hair fell into his eyes, and he brushed it back with a practised gesture. A man typically so groomed looked even more unhinged, with his hair out of place.

"You think I don't see the way you look at him? The way you used to look at me?"

Lucy's heart raced, her breaths coming in brief gasps. "Graham, please, you're being ridiculous. You don't need to be jealous of him."

"Jealousy doesn't begin to cover it, Lucy." His voice dropped, a dangerous edge creeping in. "I hate him. For what he represents, for the past he shares with you. I hate him."

"Your jealousy is your demon, Graham," she said, her tone gaining strength. "Denny means nothing to me now."

"Nothing?" He leaned closer, their faces mere inches apart. "Then why does his name burn in my mind, keeping me awake at night?"

"Because you let it!" Her outburst surprised them both. "You're letting this—your hatred—tear us apart!"

"Perhaps we were already broken," he muttered, stepping back as if her words had physically pushed him away.

"Maybe we are," Lucy conceded, her voice barely above a whisper. But as Graham turned away, hiding the mischievous glint of his eyes now darkened by shadows, she knew their argument was far from over. The tension remained.

As she watched his retreating figure, Lucy felt the weight of their fractured bond pulling her down.

Graham didn't look back before grabbing his jacket and storming out of the room.

Denny Blackwood strode onto the top deck, his footsteps silent against the thrumming of the rain. He leaned into the fierce gale that buffeted him and pulled his collar as high as it would go. Tonight's argument with Terri had been the last crack in their already shattered façade. He didn't know how they would get through the next few days.

"Stop fucking raining," he muttered to himself, squinting against the stinging spray of the ocean churned up by the storm.

The darkness was near absolute, except for the occasional flash of lightning that illuminated the deck in stark, white light. It hauntingly illuminated enormous waves in the distance.

Denny's thoughts were a chaotic whirlpool, the storm outside mirroring his turmoil. The splintering of his marriage echoed in the crashing that threatened to swallow the ship whole. As he paced the deck, each step reverberated with a heaviness that matched the burden on his shoulders.

But amidst the wind and rain, another sound cut through the chaos — footsteps, muffled yet distinct on the wet wooden planks. Denny froze, his heart quickening as he strained to catch any hint of who might be approaching.

Why was someone else here at this time of the night?

The footsteps drew closer, irregularly, like a hesitant dance on the deck. Denny's breath hitched in his throat, and a cold sweat broke out on his forehead.

Was it Terri who came to plead with him once more? Or perhaps Peter or Graham, finally wanting to confront him?

Or, indeed, another passenger seeking the isolation of a ship's deck in a storm.

A figure emerged from the shadows, barely more than a silhouette against the relentless dark.

"Rough night for a stroll, isn't it, Denny?" a voice cut through the roar of the wind, sarcastic and cold.

"Why are you here?" Denny demanded, peering into the gloom. His heart pounded, not from fear—he had never known such a thing—but from irritation.

"Tell me why you're here, and stop bloody raining!" demanded Denny, looking at the skies.

"Your authority doesn't extend to the weather or me," the voice replied, moving closer with an assuredness that irked Denny.

"Is this some kind of joke?" Denny snapped, squaring his shoulders, ready to confront the bold intruder. "I'm in no mood for games."

"I'm not in the mood for games either. I never was," the figure said, stepping into the dim glow of an emergency light. Lightning cracked overhead, but the face remained obscured, a hood casting a deep shadow over their features.

"Then why lurk in the dark? Speak your piece," Denny growled, his tone betraying his eagerness to exert control over the situation.

"Oh, I have nothing to say," the voice taunted before swiftly and unexpectedly lunging at him, the sound of fabric rustling violently against the howling wind.

Denny's reflexes were sluggish, and his body was unprepared for the assault. Usually, it would take someone powerful to overpower Denny, but his off-balance state almost made it easier for his attacker.

The figure knew they had one attempt at pushing Denny overboard to negate a struggle.

With a violent shove, Denny felt his feet slip beneath him, his balance vanishing as quickly as his hopes of overpowering his opponent. His back hit the railing with a sickening thud, the metal cold and unyielding against his spine. Water surged below, a maelstrom waiting with open jaws.

Denny's body hit the icy water, and his splash quickly disappeared into the darkness along the ship's side.

The figure stood alone, watching the spot where Denny had disappeared. No words were spoken; none were needed. The deed was done, and the sea would keep its secrets.

Denny did not reappear above the surface, and none of his cries were heard.

Whether the impact on the sea killed Denny or the cold of the North Sea, Denny was dead.

CHAPTER EIGHT

SUNDAY MORNING

THE EMERALD EMPRESS

DAY TWO OF THE CRUISE

Morning dawned with an ominous grey light filtering through the portholes. The light constantly changed as the sun tried unsuccessfully to poke through the clouds, like someone was outside, fading up and down a dimmer switch at random. The friends stirred uneasily in their beds, the tension from the night before lingering like a bad dream. Each one taunted themselves with things they should and shouldn't have said. Most were now almost used to the constant swaying of the ship in the uneasy waters.

It was Terri's frantic screams that jarred everyone awake.

"He's gone!" she cried, her voice cracking under the weight of panic as she burst into the dining room where the other two couples had gathered in hopes of a calming breakfast.

"Denny didn't come back last night!"

Two chairs remained empty at the group's breakfast table as Sarah, Lucy, Peter, and Graham started on the warm pastries from the breakfast buffet. The clatter of silverware hitting plates reverberated loudly as heads turned and faces paled. A typically composed man, Peter stood so abruptly that his chair toppled backwards.

"What do you mean gone?" he demanded, alarm etching deep lines across his placid brow.

"Missing," Terri repeated, her eyes wild as they darted from one shocked face to another.

"I've told the captain. Terri gestured to the man standing with her in full uniform. They're starting a search, inside and out. He went out for a walk. I fell asleep."

"He would have just passed out somewhere, drunk. He used to do it all the time. Check all the sofas on the ship." Graham looked unconcerned, still looking at the croissant he was applying butter to.

The ship's captain, Gerald Edwards, stood at Terri's side. He was dressed in his full uniform, which was nothing official, primarily for show on the ship, letting everyone know he was the captain.

"Search? Outside?" Sarah echoed, her hand flying to her head.

"In this storm?"

"Impossible," Graham muttered under his breath, though loud enough for Lucy beside him to hear. She gave him a sharp look, her concern morphing into suspicion at his tone.

"Let's not jump to conclusions," Lucy suggested, her voice measured but unable to hide the tremor of fear beneath it. It felt like something that she should say.

"He might have found shelter somewhere on deck."

"Shelter? Have you seen the waves crashing outside?" Terri spat, her anger momentarily overtaking her worry. Her green eyes blazed with an intensity that made even the stalwart captain flinch.

"Mrs. Blackwood is correct; we are searching the whole interior of the ship; the storm won't impact that," the captain interjected, stepping forward with some authority.

"We are doing all we can, but we must prepare ourselves for... various outcomes. We don't have CCTV for every part of the ship." He said, trying to sound positive.

"But we do have footage of Mr Blackwood going out onto deck but not returning, although, as I say, there are blind spots, some exits to the deck that we can't access, so we can't be completely sure he didn't come back in.

We have notified the authorities on land, but we have an on-board investigation team on the ship. They can't send anyone out to us until the storm dies."

"Various outcomes?" Terri echoed hollowly, her voice barely above a whisper now. "You think he's—"

"Terri, we don't know anything yet," Sarah said quickly, reaching out to touch Terri's arm in a rare gesture of solidarity.

"Let's organise ourselves," Peter suggested, trying to take charge, but unconvincingly.

"Form search parties. Cover every inch of this ship."

"Good idea," Graham agreed, though his glance with Lucy spoke of unvoiced fears.

"Everyone, please remain calm," the captain urged, raising his hands. "Panic will only hinder our efforts. Let's proceed systematically. My team is searching the ship, so I can only suggest we remain calm. You won't be able to help us."

"Remain calm," Terri repeated numbly, looking around at the concerned faces. "Right."

"Where were you last night, Terri?" Sarah asked gently, her curiosity tinged with concern.

"In our room, alone," Terri answered, her gaze dropping to the floor.

"I fell asleep waiting for him."

"Alone?" Graham queried, a hint of doubt seeping into his voice. "All night?"

"Are you insinuating something?" Terri snapped, her head snapping up, eyes flashing dangerously.

"Easy," Lucy cut in, glancing nervously between the two. "This won't find Denny."

"Indeed," the captain said firmly, almost embarrassed that he was in danger of getting involved in a discussion containing the tensions of the group. "Let us focus on the search. Time is important."

As everyone dispersed, whispers filled the air, each carrying a blend of worry, speculation, and the unspoken thought, one passenger knew the truth: they had murdered him.

Lucy's fingers trembled as she clasped them tightly in her lap. Even with the constant crackle of the storm outside, their room felt suffocating.

She glanced at Graham, who was pacing back and forth like a caged animal.

"Stop that," she hissed. "You're making me nervous."

"Where even the fuck are we?" Graham looked out of the porthole in their room at a never-ending expanse of sea.

The suffocating isolation of being surrounded by endless murky water consumed him. The absence of any sight of land pierced him like a sharp blade, leaving him trembling with fear and despair.

Graham halted mid-stride, turning to face Lucy with eyes that darted around the room before settling on her. "We need to be clear about this, Lucy. No one can know I was out last night."

"Of course," Lucy said, though the quiver in her voice betrayed her anxiety. "But if they ask—"

"They won't," he cut her off sharply. "And even if they do, we were together. All night. Remember?"

"Right," she whispered, nodding as though to convince herself. "Together all night."

"I had nothing to do with this, sweetheart; I wasn't even on the same part of the ship as him," Graham reassured her.

"How do you know?" Lucy fired back.

A knock at the door interrupted them, and their heads snapped towards the sound. A voice called from the other side, "Mr. and Mrs. Winslow, ship security. May we have a word?"

"Play it cool," Graham muttered under his breath as he strode to the door and opened it with a practised smile.

Two stern-faced men entered, one in a crisp uniform and the other in plain clothes, with a badge clipped to his belt.

"We apologise for the intrusion," the uniformed officer began.

"We're questioning all guests regarding Mr. Blackwood's disappearance."

"Of course," Graham said smoothly. "Ask away."

"Where were you both last evening after the dinner party?" the plain clothes detective inquired, pulling out a small notepad.

"We do have jurisdiction over this matter while on board. I'm an ex-detective but work for the cruise line. It's an international water kind of thing. Do you have any questions about that?"

"No, of course not. We just want to help," replied Lucy.

"So, where were you after you left the dinner last night?" the detective asked again.

"In here, with each other," Graham answered promptly, reassuringly touching Lucy's shoulder.

"Can anyone confirm that?" the detective pressed, glancing between them.

"Confirm?" Lucy echoed, her heart pounding. "We didn't think we'd need an alibi for staying in our room together."

"We're not into that kind of thing," Graham sniggered, expecting approval from the officers. Lucy threw him a disapproving look; this was not a time for jokes, which Graham always struggled with.

"Alibi is a strong word, Mrs. Winslow. We're just making some enquiries so everyone can remember what happened last night. We'll pass this on to the authorities on land," the ship's detective said, softening his tone slightly.

"Very well," the officer said, snapping his notebook shut.

"I appreciate your cooperation. We'll contact you if we have any further questions."

As he closed his notebook, he glanced down and saw some notes he had made yesterday about problems they'd been having with the CCTV system.

A cruise ship of that size didn't need a full-time crime investigator; this was an add-on duty to his usual technical duties, maintaining the ship's IT systems.

"Oh, just one more thing," he said, "do either of you own a red hoody? People have told us someone was walking around in a red hoody with the hood up late last night. We haven't been able to identify them. I'm sure it's nothing, but it would be good to eliminate them."

"Uh, no," said Graham, looking at Lucy for confirmation, "neither of us does."

With a curt nod, the two officers left the room, their departure as sudden as their arrival.

As soon as the door clicked shut, Graham released his hold on Lucy's shoulder and began to pace the room. "Lucy, I hate this. I can't prove I wasn't involved, but I will come under even more suspicion as soon as I lie about my whereabouts."

Lucy nodded, her hands trembling slightly as she clasped them together.

"Graham, this is getting serious. If they find out, you were out last night.."

"Shh," Graham interrupted, his eyes scanning the room's corners as though expecting hidden ears in the shadows.

"We agreed, remember? It's our little secret. Besides, it's not as if I had anything to do with what happened.

I probably wasn't even on the same part of the boat as him. They haven't got CCTV everywhere, the captain said that, but they'll see that if they need to. I didn't go out on that deck."

"Of course, it's our secret," Lucy whispered, but her gaze fell to the carpet, unable to meet his. Why did he keep mentioning a deck?

She hated the lies that seemed to spill so easily from her lips, but the thought of exposing Graham's midnight wanderings—and whatever else he might be hiding—terrified her even more.

"Good. Now, let's go join the others," Graham said, straightening his collar. "We mustn't appear antisocial or, God forbid, guilty. We're not guilty."

Lucy didn't reply, but gathered her suit jacket.

They exited their suite to find the corridor bustling with activity. Crew members moved briskly, their faces etched with concern, while guests whispered in hushed tones, casting furtive glances at each passing officer. The ship's staff carried radios that crackled at different volumes.

"Left-upper deck clear," was something Lucy heard as she passed someone.

The tension aboard the ship was palpable, like an electric current charging the air.

Lucy felt Graham's hand in the small of her back, guiding her through the crowd. His touch, once a source of comfort, now made her skin crawl, but she knew it was necessary, not just to make him feel like they were a happy couple, but to maintain that appearance to everyone else.

“Remember, darling,” Graham murmured into her ear as they descended the staircase to the main salon. “We are in this together. For better, for worse.”

“Until death parts us,” Lucy added silently to herself.

CHAPTER NINE

SUNDAY LUNCHTIME
THE EMERALD EMPRESS
DAY TWO OF THE CRUISE

The storm howled around them, its furious gusts clawing at the ship's steel frame, making the modern vessel creak and groan. Rain pelted the windows in relentless torrents, and lightning seared the churning skies occasionally, casting ghostly shadows across the faces of the worried guests gathered in the expansive, electrically lit room. Word had spread around most of the guests on board, who looked in the direction of the people who knew Denny.

Edward Smythe, who felt like he should be there for the group, joined Sarah, Lucy, Graham, Terri, and Peter.

"Have you seen anything like this before?" Sarah asked, gesturing to the window, her voice barely audible above the storm's roar. She wrapped her arms around herself, seeking comfort in the warmth that seemed to elude the room.

"Only once," Edward Smythe replied, his eyes mirroring the flash of lightning outside, "on a voyage many years ago. But even then, not with such... ferocity and not lasting this long."

"Nor with a man gone missing," Graham added sharply, his words slicing through the din. His gaze swept the room, resting momentarily on each of his companions.

"We must consider every possibility. Denny was troubled last night—more than usual."

"Troubled enough to wander into this storm?" Lucy queried, her tone laced with disbelief and a slight shake of the head. She moved closer to the window, peering into the abyss as if hoping for a sign of Denny amidst the chaos, even though she knew that was ridiculous.

"If I was investigating this, so many people had a reason to hurt Denny," said Sarah, regretting it as soon as she'd said it.

"Surely you don't think one of us..." Peter began, his question unfinished in the charged atmosphere. He was surprised his wife would even suggest it.

"Who else?" Sarah countered with unexpected enthusiasm.

"We were the last to see him alive, weren't we? It's logical to assume.... We have to be honest. We all had our reasons and good ones."

"Logic has no place where emotions run high," Graham interposed, his demeanour calm and collected despite the circumstances.

"Let's not forget that we are all friends here. Or at least, we should be."

"Friends don't keep secrets from each other," Lucy shot back, her eyes flaring with an intensity that belied her usual composure. Her glance strayed to Graham, who met her stare unflinchingly.

"Perhaps now is not the time for accusations. You're all upset," Edward Smythe suggested diplomatically, though his piercing expression hinted at the wheels turning behind his calm exterior.

"We should focus on finding Denny—if he can still be found."

The group fell silent, each lost in turbulent thoughts as the storm raged on, indifferent to human concerns. Slowly, one by one, they looked towards Terri. Even though she had been unhappy, she had still lost her husband.

"I'm going back to my room," declared Terri. "I need to be on my own."

The friends nodded and sat silently, running through their thoughts in isolation. They all knew they hadn't been as sensitive as they should be in her presence.

As Terri walked into her dimly lit cabin, she felt a shiver wash over her as the air con in the room went through her. But she also felt determined. She couldn't just sit idly by while uncertainty and fear gripped them all. With steady resolve, she made her way to the wardrobe in the corner to grab a jumper, her fingers trembling slightly as she pushed aside her clothes.

Then she saw a flash of bright colour amidst the sea of fabric. Terri's breath caught in her throat as she pulled out a bright red hoody, its vibrant hues stark against the muted tones around it. This wasn't hers or Denny's; she was sure of it.

The officers on board had mentioned the red hoody to her, too.

Terri hurried back into the salon with her heart thudding, where the others silently sat. Bursting through the doors, she shouted, "I've found something!"

They all rushed back to the Blackwood's room and crowded inside.

The sharp contrast between the opulent interior and the chaos outside was disquieting. Edward Smythe went straight to the closet as if owning the ship gave him jurisdiction to do whatever he wanted. He pushed aside the clothes to reveal a crumpled red hoody.

“Isn't this Denny's?” he asked, holding it out for the others to see.

“No,” Terri replied quickly—perhaps too quickly. “He hates red or any bright colours. He just wore black all the bloody time. I’ve never seen it before. It must belong to someone else.” Her eyes flitted nervously among the faces gathered around her.

“Wore? As in past tense?” Graham said smugly, believing he had caught her out.

“Yes, he wore only black, as in before today,” Terri started to cry.

“Bloody hell, Graham, leave it out,” even this was strong for Peter to say.

“Curiouser and curiouser,” muttered Sarah, examining the hoody. “Then why's it here?”

“Perhaps we should inform the captain,” Graham suggested, his eyes locked on Terri's face, searching for something unseen.

“Wait!” Terri's voice rose in pitch, and everyone turned to look at her.

"No more secrets, right? That's what we said." She took a deep breath, steadying herself. "I can't stand any more sly comments," she glared at Graham. "Last night, Denny and I argued."

"An argument?" Lucy echoed, her brow furrowing. "You didn't mention that before."

"It was nothing," Terri insisted, though her voice trembled slightly. "Just the same old things, same old arguments. It'd be weirder if we didn't argue last night."

"Nothing?" Lucy repeated sceptically. "It seems rather significant, given the circumstances."

Terri knew what she had secretly known all along: she didn't truly have any friends in the room.

The presence of the red hoody was a tangible clue, but its significance remained a mystery, and they did not know if it was even related, but if it wasn't Terri's.. Someone had put it there.

The ship creaked and moaned ominously as they stood there, a reminder of the relentless storm outside. The rain hammering the sides of the boat sounded almost normal now.

"Whatever happened to Denny," Terri said at last, her voice barely above a whisper but breaking the silence, "it's clear we're dealing with something darker than an accident. I had nothing to do with it, and I've never seen this hoody before."

"Indeed," Graham agreed solemnly. "We are now part of a murder investigation, whether we like it or not."

"I think I'm going to try to have a sleep," said Terri.

Peter gestured to Sarah, "We'll leave you to it."

Both couples left Terri to be alone with her thoughts and returned to their rooms.

"Knowing Denny, he'll probably show up having played a joke on us all," Graham whispered to Peter, who gave him a disapproving look at yet another ill-timed comment.

CHAPTER TEN

TWENTY YEARS EARLIER
COLLEGE PARK

A warm breeze rustled the leaves overhead as Lucy, Graham, Denny, Alice, Sarah, and Peter gathered around a picnic table in the park, just as they had done countless times during their college days. The sun cast dappled shadows on the worn wooden surface, evoking a sense of nostalgia as laughter filled the air. They had decided this would be the perfect location for a goodbye lunch before Denny and Alice would travel to New York to start what would become their new life together.

"Where is it? Where is it?" Peter said as he scoured the table's surface, moving things covering it.

"Here it is!" shouted Lucy, secretly knowing Peter knew where it was all along, but wanted to make a bit of theatre around searching for it.

The remaining five individuals leaned forward in their seats, their bodies rising in unison as they eagerly strained to get a closer look at the area of interest. Their eyes widened with curiosity.

The letters L, S, A, D, G, and P were deeply etched into the surface of the wooden table, a permanent reminder of the group's first few months at college together. The once sharp lines had now blurred and faded, mirroring the changes and growth the group had experienced. Memories flooded as they ran their fingers over the worn grooves–late-night study sessions, laughter-filled meals, and heartfelt conversations that bonded them. The table bore witness to their journey, a testament to their enduring friendship.

The group all smiled as they looked at the letters, then briefly at each other.

"Remember when we used to meet here every week?" Lucy asked, her eyes catching the sunlight. "It feels like it was just yesterday."

"Time flies. It's been 3 years," Sarah agreed, smiling warmly at the others. She brushed a strand of hair from her face, revealing eyes that held kindness.

As they enjoyed their lunch, the conversation turned to how each couple had found their way to one another. Unable to resist the opportunity for some playful teasing, Graham turned his mischievous gaze on Denny.

"Ah, Denny," he began, chuckling. "You certainly had your share of… adventures back then, didn't you?"

Denny shot him a glare, his blue eyes narrowing in annoyance. "What's your point, Graham?"

"Nothing, nothing," Graham replied, feigning innocence. He adjusted his tailored suit jacket, the picture of sophistication, even at twenty-three years old.

"I merely find it fascinating how fate works, don't you?"

Alice leaned forward, eager to share her story. "Well, Denny and I had our fair share of ups and downs," she admitted, her voice full of warmth and sincerity. "But eventually, we found our way back to each other, and I couldn't be happier."

A subtle shift in Lucy's demeanour betrayed her discomfort with the subject, but she smiled politely. She glanced at Denny, who seemed to avoid her eyes and an uneasy tension between them.

"Speaking of fate," Peter chimed in, as always hoping to ease the atmosphere, "Sarah and I met at the library, of all places. She was the only one who could make sense of my handwriting when we worked on reports together."

"Love at first sight," Sarah confirmed, her eyes twinkling with affection as she looked at her husband.

"Or love at first scribble, as it were," Peter joked, earning a polite laugh from the group. He was never one for the funniest of jokes, but it didn't stop him trying, and that was almost funnier than the jokes themselves. The group often said he was making dad jokes before becoming a dad.

As they continued to reminisce, the tension between Lucy and Denny grew increasingly palpable. The sun dipped lower in the sky, casting long shadows across the park. As the meeting neared its end, it seemed that every passing moment held the potential for secrets to be revealed.

The group had now stood up and started to mingle in pairs. As laughter echoed through the air, Denny found his gaze drawn to Sarah, who smiled at something Peter had said. He couldn't help but feel a pang of longing, knowing that he needed to talk to her about their past, which they had both never really discussed.

"Sarah," Denny called softly, hoping to catch her attention without drawing the others' notice. "Could I speak with you for a moment? Alone?"

He gestured with his head away from the group.
"Of course," she replied, concern flickering as she followed him to a secluded spot beneath a nearby tree.
"Look, I just wanted to say... I'm sorry," Denny began haltingly, his voice heavy with emotion. "I know we've all come a long way since we started college; there's water under the bridge, but I can't help thinking about everything I told you about, my troubled upbringing and how it's affected me, and I never apologised. You listened to me, you were kind to me, and I treated you like that. I did that; I'll never forgive myself. We were drunk."
"I was," Sarah replied.
Sarah then listened attentively, her nurturing nature shining through as she reached to place a comforting hand on his arm.
"Denny, we all have our struggles. You're not alone in that. Let's forget about it. I've spent a lot of time trying to forget it. This means a lot."
"I know," he sighed, studying the ground as if it held the answers to his problems. "But sometimes I worry I can't fully trust or love Alice because of it.

I've changed, I have, and you got the worst of it. I told you about what's happened in my past and my family. I like to think it doesn't affect me, but it does. I'm still so angry, Sarah; I'm sorry for how I was with you. For what I did, I can't even say it."

"Give yourself time," Sarah advised gently, her heart aching for him even as her feelings threatened to overwhelm her.

"You and Alice have been through so much together. Keep trying, and maybe you'll find that trust and love you seek. Just forget about what happened with us and promise to move on and never be like that with anyone else again."

"I won't, I promise. I've turned a corner." Said Denny genuinely.

"Promise me, Denny," Sarah needed more.

"I promise," Denny winked, which was inappropriate. Although Denny had given Sarah her worst moment in college, a moment she knew would take years to process, she knew she would get back together with him instantly, and she hated herself for it.

Meanwhile, Alice and Lucy sat side by side on a park bench. Their conversation took a serious turn as Alice opened up about her fears for her future with Denny.

"Lucy, I don't know what to do," Alice confided, tears glistening. "Denny's been struggling with depression and anger management again, you know, like he always has, and I'm worried about what that means for us."

"New York could be just the fresh start you both need," Lucy suggested, her voice full of sympathy. "It might not be easy, but don't give up on him yet. You two have something special, and I believe it can improve."

"Thank you, Lucy," Alice whispered, grateful for her friend's support. "I'll keep trying. For both of us."

Riddled with secrets, Lucy said what she thought she should say, not what she wanted to say. For her selfish reasons, she wanted them to move to New York and never come back.

Graham adjusted his bow tie, a playful glint in his eyes as he looked around at the group of friends gathered beneath the sprawling canopy of the oak tree. Their laughter and light banter could not quite mask the undercurrent of tension that had been present throughout the day.

"Ah, now here's a man who truly appreciates the finer things in life," Denny remarked, nodding toward Graham with an almost mocking smile.

"Only you, my friend, would wear a bow tie to a picnic, and it looks ok!"
"Come now, Denny," Graham replied with a good-natured chuckle. "It never hurts to add a touch of class to any occasion." He felt the subtle sting of Denny's words but brushed it off, refusing to let the barb taint the moment. He also knew that if you wore a bow tie in your early twenties, a few comments were fair enough.
"Alright, everyone, I'd like to propose a toast." Graham stood, raising his glass above the chequered tablecloth while the others followed suit.
"To the memories we've made, the bonds we've forged, and the love that ties us all together. May our friendship endure through all the trials and triumphs life offers, and good luck to Alice and Denny in the Big Apple! Don't come back too soon."
Denny winked at the slight jibe, and the group laughed.
But as the sun dipped even lower in the sky, Graham couldn't help but feel a sense of foreboding gnawing at his insides.

He watched as Denny and Sarah exchanged a loaded glance, the unspoken words passing between them like a secret language only they could decipher. Graham was jealous of Sarah's look at Denny.

"Is everything alright?" Lucy asked him, her brow furrowed with concern as she noted his sudden introspection.

"Of course," Graham lied, forcing a smile. "I'm just taking it all in–one of those 'stop and smell the roses' moments."

"Good," Lucy replied, her features softening as she leaned in for a kiss.

As their lips met, Graham couldn't shake the nagging feeling that something was amiss–a suspicion that threatened to fracture their fragile peace throughout the day. Though he didn't yet know what lay beneath their laughter and clinking glasses, he knew one thing: The truth always finds a way to rise, no matter how deep it's buried.

"New York sounds amazing," Peter said, genuine surprise clear in his warm hazel eyes. "It's quite a change from here."

"Indeed," Denny replied, allowing a hint of pride to lace his voice.

"We've been looking for a fresh start, and this opportunity came up. Alice has a new job waiting for her, and I'll take over a branch of my company there."

"What do you even do again?" Graham enquired, not satisfied with any answer he'd been given so far.

"I'm a consultant, go into companies, suggest things, mainly work with directors,"

"Wow, New York and a made-up job, living the dream!" Graham had crossed the line.

Alice chimed in, holding Denny's arm, her voice trembling slightly under the weight of the news. "We'll miss you all, but we promise to stay in touch."

A mixture of emotions rippled through the group—happiness for their friends' new adventure, envy over the thrilling unknown that awaited them, and all-out appreciation that this felt like an end to a chapter in their lives. Given the choice, most of them would choose not to see each other again.

"Here's to new beginnings," Graham said, raising his nearly empty glass again. The others followed suit, clinking their glasses together in a final salute to friendship.

"Same time next year?" Sarah suggested.

"Absolutely," Denny agreed, his voice charged with the unspoken knowledge of how much could change in a year and that they almost certainly wouldn't ever see this group of friends again. "We wouldn't miss it for the world."

As the goodbyes began, Sarah reached for Peter's hand, intertwining their fingers tightly. There was solace in his steady grip, a quiet reassurance that they would face whatever lay ahead. She thought this might be the last time she saw Denny, and she was happy that he had apologised and was committed to changing his ways. In that moment of vulnerability, they exchanged a silent vow to support one another through the changes and challenges that lurked on the horizon.

"Take care, Denny," Sarah said, her voice betraying the conflicted emotions beneath her calm exterior. "And good luck!"

"Thank you, Sarah," Denny replied, his gaze lingering just a moment too long before he turned to embrace Peter in farewell.

"Peter," Sarah whispered, gently squeezing his hand, "thank you for making me feel safe."

He smiled warmly at her, brushing a stray lock of hair from her forehead.

"Always, Sarah. You know I'm here for you, no matter what."

As they strolled toward their car, Peter couldn't help but notice the tension still clinging to Sarah. It was a palpable undercurrent that threatened to spill over into their lives, and he wondered whether the others sensed it, too.

"Did you see the way Denny looked at us?" Sarah asked suddenly, her voice wavering slightly. "Do you think he knows?"

"About what?" Peter replied, feigning nonchalance while inwardly bracing himself for her response.

"Never mind," she murmured, shaking her head. "It's nothing."

His heart pounded in his chest, a cacophony of fears and questions drumming against his ribcage.

"Sarah," Peter said softly, pausing just before they reached their car. "We'll figure this out. Whatever it is, we're in this together. I'll make it right."

"I'm not done with Denny."

She nodded, tears glistening in the corners of her eyes. "I know, Peter. And I'm grateful for that. It's hard sometimes to keep all these secrets inside."

"Maybe one day we won't have to," he offered, his voice laced with unusual vengeance. "But for now, let's focus on us and the life we're building together."

With a deep breath, Sarah mustered a small smile and leaned into Peter's embrace. As they stood in the dim light, it was as if the rest of the world had faded away, leaving only the two of them, hand in hand, fighting the darkness that threatened to engulf them.

Graham stood in the almost invisible shadow of a tall oak tree, watching Sarah and Peter walk away hand in hand. He felt longing and regret, secret thoughts of a life he would never have with Sarah disappearing away from him.

"Thoughtful, are we?" Lucy's voice interrupted his reverie. He turned to face her; his expression carefully composed.

"Merely reflecting on the day," he replied, forcing a smile. "It's been quite an eventful reunion, hasn't it?"

"Indeed," Lucy agreed, linking her arm through his. "I hope Denny and Alice find the happiness they're seeking."

"Me too," Graham murmured, his gaze drifting back towards Sarah and Peter.

Their laughter carried on the breeze, wrapping around him like a cruel reminder of what could have been.

"Are you alright, darling?" Lucy asked, concern lacing her voice. "You seem rather preoccupied."

"I'm fine," he assured her, squeezing her hand gently. "Just thinking about our friends and all the changes they're going through." If only she knew the half of it, he thought bitterly.

"Change can be a good thing," Lucy mused. It may be time for us to embrace some changes of our own.

"Perhaps," Graham conceded.

"Come on," Lucy urged, pulling him toward their car. "Let's go home,"

As they drove away, Graham stole one last glance at the picnic bench, disappearing into darkness.

"Goodbye, Sarah," he whispered under his breath, the words tasting bittersweet on his tongue. He knew he must let go of his attachment to her and focus on the life he had built with Lucy, but the thought of releasing those feelings felt impossible.

CHAPTER ELEVEN

THE EMERALD EMPRESS

SUNDAY EVENING

DAY TWO OF THE CRUISE

Lucy knocked softly on the door, her knuckles barely whispering against the polished mahogany. The silence that followed felt like it had lasted a lifetime, and an unease settled between her and Sarah as they waited outside Terri's room. With a click, the door slowly swung inward, revealing Terri's room bathed in the dim glow of evening light filtering through the sheer curtains.

Terri, usually known for her immaculate appearance, stood in front of them wearing baggy, mismatched pyjamas. Her hair was dishevelled, and she had dark circles under her eyes, giving her an uncharacteristically unkempt but still beautiful appearance.

"Terri?" Lucy's voice gently invaded the quiet space. "It's been a few hours. We thought we'd check on you."

"Of course, come in," the reply said, though it lacked its usual warmth. Terri stood by the window, her silhouette tense against the waning light.

Lucy stepped into the room, with Sarah close behind. Their heels clicked on the hardwood floor before they reached the plush carpet. They found Terri clutching her arms as if holding herself together.

"Terri, are you alright?" Sarah's concern wrapped around her words like a soft shawl.

A brittle laugh escaped Terri's lips before she could clamp it down.

"Alright? Oh, I'm far better than alright." Her green eyes flashed, not with tears, but with something harder to define. "Denny's dead, I know it."

The words hung in the air, a stark declaration that echoed off the walls.

Lucy and Sarah exchanged glances, and a silent conversation passed between them. Their look spoke volumes: confusion, fear, suspicion—all mingling in the space of a heartbeat.

"Terri, you can't mean that," Lucy finally said, stepping closer. Her typically composed features were tight with worry.

"Can't I?" Terri's gaze was unwavering. "After all, he put me through—the lies, the manipulation, the hurt—I should be mourning, shouldn't I? But no, I feel... liberated. I'm free." She let out a shaky breath, and for a moment, the facade cracked, revealing the raw edges of her pain.

"Relief is a natural response," Sarah offered, trying to read Terri's expression. "Especially after such a turbulent relationship. But we don't know that Denny is dead; he might be found."

"Natural or not," Lucy interjected, "it doesn't seem wise to express it so openly. People will talk, and in our current situation, any talk isn't helpful."

"Let them," Terri said, a defiant spark igniting within her. "I'm tired of hiding, of pretending. Denny's gone, and I..." She trailed off, her resolve wobbling.

"Terri," Sarah said softly, reaching out to place a comforting hand on her shoulder, "we're here for you. We always have been."

"Have you?" Terri's question pierced the air.

Lucy stepped forward, her presence commanding despite her petite frame. "We need to stick together, now more than ever. We can get through this, but only if we're united."

"United," Terri laughed, "Yes, perhaps that's what we need to be." But the smile wasn't natural; it remained guarded, like a soldier who had seen too many battles.

"Okay, well, we're going to dinner shortly. Are you going to come along?" said Sarah.

"Of course, I'm starving!" said Terri with a crazed smile. She was a woman on the edge of something.

As the door closed behind them, Lucy turned to Sarah, a crease marring her forehead—a veil of uncertainty that shrouded their shared suspicions.

"Do you believe her, Sarah?" Lucy's voice was barely above a whisper, tinged with doubt. "About being glad Denny's dead? But having nothing to do with it?"

Sarah paused in contemplation. "I don't know, Lucy. It's hard to say. Terri has always been guarded, but this... it feels different. But I suppose grief hits in different ways."

A flicker of concern crossed Lucy's features.

"What if she had something to do with it? What if—"

Sarah held up a hand, cutting off Lucy's words. "Let's not jump to conclusions just yet.

We all have our reasons for wanting Denny gone, but that doesn't make us murderers. She may be happy now, but she wouldn't have killed him." Her eyes held a steely determination.

Lucy and Sarah, their steps syncing in silent urgency, navigated the maze of corridors of the ship to find Peter and Graham. The corridors had ornate wall lamps at regular intervals, each lighting the space in front of them, meaning the light dipped until you started to reach the next. They found Graham and Peter silently ensconced in deep leather chairs facing a grand porthole.

"Peter, Graham," Lucy began, her voice betraying a tremor she couldn't suppress, "we've just spoken with Terri."

"Is she alright?" Peter asked, his eyes reflecting genuine concern as he rose to his feet.

Sarah's lips formed a rueful half-smile.

"She's... relieved that Denny's dead or missing. Actually, she seems happy," she confided, tucking a stray chestnut curl behind her ear.

"Happy?" Graham echoed, his brow furrowing into a tight lattice of disbelief. "That's a strong word under the circumstances."

"Indeed," Lucy added, "it's unsettling."

"Let's find somewhere private to talk," suggested Peter, gesturing to some nearby passengers and guiding the group away from those prying ears to a secluded corner of the ship where the murmur of conversation and the clinking of glasses from the nearby lounge became a distant echo.

Once they had settled into the shadows, Peter said, "Alright, let's lay our cards on the table. What did Denny mean to each of us? Truthfully."

Graham looked out at the dark waters beyond the porthole before speaking.

"Denny was always my rival; he always had been charismatic and successful. Everything I felt I wasn't. It gnawed at me," he admitted.

"Sarah?" Peter asked gently, turning towards his wife. He knew this was a risky question and that Sarah wouldn't be honest.

"Where do I begin?" Sarah sighed; her gaze fixed on the floor. "He was a charming monster. Charming one moment, cruel the next. He could make you feel like the only person in the world, and then..." Her voice trailed off, leaving the sentence to finish itself in the silence.

"His death doesn't exactly bring a tear to my eye," she finally confessed, lifting her eyes to meet theirs.

"But wishing him dead is one thing—being responsible for it is another."

"Lucy?" Peter's question redirected the spotlight.

"Business," Lucy said curtly, her fingers fidgeting with the hem of her sleeve. "He ruined what Sarah and I built from scratch. He had a way of twisting things, making you doubt your mind. But that's no motive for murder."

"Of course not," Graham said quickly, too quickly perhaps, as he glanced at Lucy with a mix of concern and something else—a flicker of suspicion.

"None of us are capable of killing someone, right?" Peter's statement sounded like a question, one that begged for affirmation.

"Right," they murmured in a chorus of feigned conviction.

"Then we're agreed," Sarah said, her voice steadying. "We all had reasons to dislike Denny, but none of us would act on them."

"Exactly," Lucy affirmed, though the quickened pace of her heart belied the confidence of her words.

"Good," Peter nodded, satisfied. "Because we need to trust each other if we're going to get through this."

"Trust," echoed Graham, a wry twist to his lips. "Yes, let's hope that's enough."

"So, Peter, what about you? We know he had a thing with Sarah a while back," said Graham, clearly growing nervous.

"Graham!" said Lucy in disapproval.

"No, it's ok," said Peter. "It's only fair that I answer the same question. Yes, I hate him; I mean, I hated him. I hated what he did to you. I know you haven't told me everything, but I'm okay with that. I don't need to know. I'm sorry I'm not good enough to hear it." He held out his hand to Sarah.

"But that's behind us now. We've moved on, and now he's gone."

Sarah and Peter looked at each other and exchanged a genuine smile.

"But whatever happens, we all stick together. Maybe things happen for a reason," smiled Lucy.

With their pact sealed in the dim corner, the friends clung to the fragile raft of their agreement as waves of doubt and fear lapped at its edges. As they dispersed back into the ship's social ballet, each step felt loaded, each smile more strained.

CHAPTER TWELVE

SUNDAY EVENING, DINNER
THE EMERALD EMPRESS
DAY TWO OF THE CRUISE

The guests ate in silence; Terri hadn't joined them for dinner.

The sound of measured footsteps approached, each a tap on the polished floorboards. The group shifted uneasily as Edward Smythe emerged from the other room, his hair catching the dim light like a beacon in the gloom.

"Ah, here you all are," Edward said, his voice resonating with a calm that belied the tension gripping the room. "I trust I'm not interrupting anything too... intimate?"

"Edward," Graham greeted, masking his surprise with a veneer of politeness. "To what do we owe the pleasure?"

"Business, I'm afraid," Edward replied, studying each of them with those piercing blue eyes. "It seems our little predicament has taken yet another twist."

"Predicament?" Lucy's voice betrayed a hint of nervousness. "What do you mean?"

"Terri Blackwood," Edward announced gravely, "has been taken into custody on board the ship."

"Terri?" Sarah's hand flew to her mouth, her eyes wide with disbelief. "But why? We just left her an hour or so ago,"

"Fresh evidence," Edward continued, clasping his hands behind his back. "Something quite damning has surfaced. They finished going through the hours of CCTV. I'm sure it's all standard procedure, but until this is sorted out, she'll remain under the watchful eye of the ship's security. We don't normally tell the passengers we have a holding cell on board. Spoils the fun."

"Damn it," Peter cursed under his breath. "This is madness. Terri? A murderer? I can't believe it."

"Belief often has little to do with reality," Edward remarked cryptically. "In any case, I thought you should be aware. After all, such news spreads rapidly, and I'd hate for you to be caught unawares."

"Thank you, Edward, for the warning," Graham said, his words stiff with formality.

"Indeed," Edward nodded, his gaze lingering on the group before he turned to leave. "Good evening to you all."

As Edward disappeared back into the shadows, the friends exchanged looks of confusion and dread.

"Taken into custody?" Lucy repeated, her voice a whisper of fear. "What could they have found to implicate Terri?"

"Who knows?" Sarah murmured. "But one thing's clear—none of us are safe. Not anymore."

"Then we stick to the plan," Peter said firmly. "We stay united. We protect each other."

"Until one of us gets taken away next," Graham added darkly.

"Let's not borrow trouble, why would you get taken away?" Lucy cautioned. "We need to learn more about this so-called evidence."

After the group bid farewell, Graham and Lucy returned to their suite without saying a word. Their silence continued in their room.

Graham again paced the room, his hands trembling.

"I need some air. I can't take this anymore, being cooped up in here while a killer is on the loose, there's no way Terri did it." Graham looked out the window at the churning sea and the pelting rain.

Lucy's eyes widened. "Graham, no. It's not safe out there, not after what happened to Denny. Please, stay here with me." She reached for his hand, but he pulled away.

"I'll be careful, I promise. I won't go near the edge." He grabbed his waterproof coat from the hook. "I just need a few minutes to clear my head."

Lucy bit her lip, her brow furrowed with worry. "At least take your phone. And don't be long, alright? I need you here with me."

Graham nodded curtly. The walls felt like they were closing in on him, and he felt like he was suffocating. He had to get out, even just for a moment. Lucy meant well, but she didn't understand the demons clawing at his mind.

Graham shrugged on his coat. "I'll only be a few minutes." He strode to the door, avoiding her imploring gaze, his hand pausing on the handle. Was this a mistake? He had a niggle in his head that he shouldn't go.

No, he needed this. Sucking in a sharp breath, he yanked open the door and stepped out into the cold corridor. The door clicked shut behind him with an ominous finality.

Icy tendrils of mist curled around him as he approached the deck, each footstep echoing too loudly in the eerie stillness of the corridor, but turned to a raging menace when he opened the heavy door that led out onto the deck. He glanced at the security camera above the door.

'Shouldn't there be a light on it?' he thought to himself.

Graham's feet carried him to the spot where Denny had disappeared, they had since been told which deck Denny had gone out onto. It was as if he was drawn by some morbid fascination, needing to see what Denny saw that night. The storm still raged around him, the wind howling like a wounded beast, groaning around the ship's structure. He pulled his hood up, not liking the fact that he obscured his peripheral vision. Graham felt small, and the boat felt small, a stick floating on a river at the will of nature. Sheets of rain pelted his face, stinging his eyes and blurring his vision. He gripped the railing before him but was still away from the edge, the metal cold and slick beneath his fingers.

He stared into the churning sea, the waves crashing against the hull relentlessly. What had possessed Denny to come out here? And when he did, had he been pushed? Had he jumped? Had he slipped?

The questions swirled in Graham's mind, taunting him with their lack of answers.

As his eyes adjusted to the darkness, a different flicker of movement caught his attention. In the moonlight, there was the unmistakable shape. A figure stood at the other end of the deck, with its back to Graham. His heart seized in his chest. It couldn't be...

“Denny?” he whispered; his voice stolen by the wind.

The figure slowly turned, and Graham stared into the spectral face of his friend. Denny's lips curled into a terrifying smile, but there was something wrong about it, something twisted and unnatural, a smile Graham had never seen before.

“This isn’t real,” Graham whispered to himself.

Denny's arm rose, his finger beckoning Graham to come closer. Graham's feet moved of their own accord, drawn to the phantom like a moth to a flame.

The rational part of his mind screamed at him to turn back and run, but he couldn't tear himself away like he was in a dream, couldn’t control his actions, and couldn’t scream.

As he neared the edge, Denny's smile widened as if pleased with Graham's progress. Then, without warning, the figure leapt over the side, vanishing into the roiling waves below without a splash.

Graham lurched forward, a strangled cry tearing from his throat. "Denny, no!"

But it was too late. The deck was empty; the only sound was the howling of the wind, cancelling everything else. Had it been real?

He leaned over the side to look at the swirling waves below him.

"DENNY!" he cried into the void.

He focussed on a wave that seemed to have an unnatural shape on it.

Then, inch by inch, Denny's head and shoulders slowly emerged from the dark, churning wave, the grin on his face still wide and unnatural, stretching into something Graham had never seen before. His eyes, oh those eyes, glassy and unblinking, locked onto Graham's with a soulless intensity, but they were as black as the darkest night.

Without shifting its arms, the figure began gliding back toward the ship, its movements smooth and inhuman, as if dragged by unseen hands beneath the surface.

The surrounding water rippled and hissed as if whispering secrets of the deep, each one more menacing than the last.

Graham stumbled back from the railing, his legs trembling beneath him.

Graham knew he couldn't leave at this point. He needed to prove to himself that he had just been seeing things.

He slowly walked back over to the ship's edge and forced himself through squinting eyes to look back towards where he had seen the figure. To his relief, there was nothing there. He breathed a vast sigh of relief and chuckled to himself.

With two hands on the railing, he instinctively looked down the ship's side.

His gaze was again met by the smiling figure climbing the vessel's side. Silent shrieks screamed through his mind, and as if in a nightmare, he could only turn and run in slow motion.

His feet wouldn't move as they should. He slipped on the deck and fell to his knees. His feet clawed at the deck, trying to get traction, waiting for something to grab his ankle.

He had to get back inside, back to the safety of his cabin, and back to Lucy. He couldn't let her see him like this or tell her the depths of his unravelling.

Graham turned and ran, his feet still slipping on the wet deck. The steps loomed ahead, and in his haste, he missed one, his ankle twisting painfully beneath him. Although everything was still loud, he heard the crack. He cried out, tumbling down the remaining stairs in a tangle of limbs.

Pain shot through his leg as he struggled to his feet, but the fear coursing through his veins propelled him forward. He limped along the corridor, his breath coming in ragged gasps. The shadows seemed to reach for him, dark fingers grasping at his heels. He didn't want to look behind.

"It's not real," he muttered, his voice lost in the emptiness of the hallways. "It can't be real."

But the memory of Denny's ghostly smile, the beckoning finger, and the plunge into the abyss played on a loop in his mind, taunting and mocking him. He glanced over his shoulder, half expecting to see the spectre following close behind, but nothing.

The door to his cabin appeared like a beacon of salvation. Graham stumbled forward, his fists pounding against the wood. "Lucy!" he cried, his voice breaking. "Lucy, please, open the door!"

Seconds stretched into an eternity before the door swung open, revealing Lucy's concerned face. “Graham? What's wrong? What happened?”

He fell into her arms, his body shaking, wet and lifeless. He was unravelling.

Lucy held him close, stroking his hair as she murmured soothing words. But even as she comforted him, a flicker of something dark crossed her face, gone so quickly he might have imagined it.

“It's okay,” she whispered. “You're safe now. Everything will be all right.”

CHAPTER THIRTEEN

TEN YEARS EARLIER
LA ROSERAIE RESTAURANT

Lucy Winslow eased into the plush velvet chair at a secluded corner table at La Roseraie restaurant. The flickering candlelight cast shadows that danced across her delicate features. She tilted her head slightly, offering Sarah Emerson, who sat opposite her, a practised smile.

"Sarah, darling, you look beautiful, as always." Lucy's voice was a soft purr wrapped in silk, betraying none of the tension that coiled within her like a spring. She knew a serious conversation needed to happen at this dinner and wanted to get to it as quickly as possible. Sarah appreciated the compliment, but always knew Lucy thought she looked better.

"Lucy, thank you," Sarah replied. "And you are the very picture of elegance tonight." Her tone was warm, yet a cautious note hovered beneath the surface, like a delicate frost on spring blooms.

The two women exchanged smiles, each painted with the artistry of socialites skilled in concealing their genuine sentiments. Their laughter mingled with the low hum of conversation from nearby tables.

"Another successful soirée last night," Lucy remarked, tilting her head to study Sarah's reaction. "It's remarkable how we manage it all, isn't it?"

"Truly," Sarah agreed, her fingers tracing the stem of her wine glass. "Though I must admit, it takes its toll."

"Indeed," Lucy murmured, her gaze lingering on Sarah's hand, noting how it trembled ever so slightly. "Sometimes I wonder if it's all worth it—the strain it puts not just on our time, but on... friendships, too."

The word stayed between them, the first blow in an inevitable conflict. Sarah's eyes flickered with a shadow of something more profound, perhaps regret or a secret unease. Lucy watched the corners of her mouth twitching imperceptibly as she registered each minute shift in Sarah's demeanour.

"Friendships," Sarah echoed, the word escaping like a sigh, "are complicated, aren't they? They require patience... and forgiveness."

"Forgiveness," Lucy repeated softly, her heart thrumming in her chest as she leaned forward, hands folded neatly on the table. "Such a precious commodity these days." Her voice remained even, but a glint in her eye betrayed the storm beneath her calm exterior.

"Lucy, what—" Sarah started, then paused, her expression tightening. "Is everything alright?"

"Of course," Lucy replied too quickly, her smile fixed as she brushed an imaginary speck from her dress.

"Why wouldn't it be?" She looked at Sarah from the side of her eyes and drank her wine.

For a moment, neither woman spoke. The restaurant's ambient noise swelled around them.

With ambitious hearts and a shared vision, the pair had launched their business just two years prior. They began by organising small business conferences, but their success propelled them into high-end event coordination. The opulent world of exclusive parties and extravagant gatherings was now their playground; they revelled in every moment. What started as a hobby was now earning more money than each of their husbands made.

Their meticulous planning and attention to detail set them apart from others in the industry, making them the go-to choice for the most discerning clients. As they sat back and admired their latest masterpiece, they couldn't help but feel a sense of pride and accomplishment for how far they had come in just a short time.

Despite the challenges that often arose while working with a friend, they agreed to prioritise their friendship. And so, whenever they hosted a successful event, they would come together for a celebratory dinner, reminiscing on their most recent success. For them, it was about business or success and nurturing and appreciating their relationship. The dinners were filled with laughter, stories, and promises to continue supporting each other's dreams and endeavours. It was a reminder that no matter what obstacles came their way, their friendship would always remain strong and unbreakable, or so they thought.

"Lucy," Sarah began again, her voice lower, more insistent, "if there's something—"

"Let's not spoil our evening, shall we?" Lucy cut in, her tone light but carrying an edge sharp enough to draw blood. "After all, life is too short for anything less than perfect evenings."

"Of course," Sarah acquiesced, her spine straightening like bracing against an unseen force. "Perfect evenings."

Lucy swirled the wine in her glass, thinking, watching the ruby liquid catch the flickering candlelight. "Our little venture has taken off, hasn't it?" she remarked, a note of pride threading through her words.

"Beyond our wildest dreams," Sarah agreed, "But these meals are the only time we talk."

"Ah," Lucy sighed, setting down her glass with a soft clink. "The price of success."

"Perhaps too steep a price for friendship," Sarah ventured, her gaze steady on Lucy's face.

There was a pause.

Lucy tapped her fingers on the table, a rhythm that filled the momentary silence.

"Speaking of prices," Lucy began, her tone casual but probing, "I bumped into Denny the other day."

"Did you?" Sarah's response was carefully neutral, but her hand tightened imperceptibly around her fork. She felt sick at the mention of his name.

"Yes, imagine my surprise," Lucy continued, her eyes locked onto Sarah's. "He seemed... different. He talked about you a lot. He didn't mention abandoning Alice in New York and coming home."

Sarah shifted in her seat; her smile strained. "People change, Lucy. It's the nature of life."

"Indeed, they do," Lucy pressed on, leaning in just a fraction closer. "But some things remain constant, don't they? Like secrets."

"Lucy—" Sarah's voice wavered for the first time, betraying a hint of vulnerability.

"Please, Sarah," Lucy implored softly, yet with an undercurrent of steel. "No more secrets between us."

The two women held each other's gazes for a long moment, anticipating the impending revelation. Finally, Sarah exhaled, a breath she had held in for far too long.

"Alright," she conceded, her shoulders slumping as if unburdening herself of a great weight. "It's true. I was seeing Denny, again."

The confession fell like a tumbling stone between them.

"You and Denny?" Her voice trembled, barely above a whisper, as if the words themselves were fragile things that might crumble under the weight of her betrayal.

"Lucy, I—"

"Stop." Lucy raised a hand, her slender fingers trembling in the dim light. "How long?"

"Six months, but don't hate me. It wasn't good. He wasn't good to me," Sarah murmured, what she said not even making sense, her hair falling like a curtain to hide her shame.

"Six months," Lucy repeated hollowly. The surrounding chatter grew louder, a metallic chorus witnessing her heart fracturing. She could feel the eyes of other diners on them, drawn by the moment's impact. Their hushed murmurs added a backdrop to the unfolding drama.

"Lucy, please understand—"

"Understand?" Anger seeped into Lucy's voice, breaking through the sadness. "You knew how I feel about him. How could you?"

Sarah's gaze finally lifted, meeting Lucy's stormy eyes. "It wasn't planned. It just... happened. I didn't mean to hurt you."

"Didn't mean to—" But Lucy's retort was cut short as the waiter approached, oblivious to the tension. He refilled their water glasses with a smile, then retreated, leaving behind an uneasy silence.

"Did Peter know?" Lucy asked once they were alone again, her voice gaining strength as she struggled to piece together the remnants of her composure.

Sarah shook her head, her hands clasped tightly in her lap. “No. Nobody knew. It was a mistake, Lucy. One I regret every day. Peter knows now.”

“Regret?” Lucy's laugh held no humour, the sound jagged and brittle. “That's easy for you to say now, right?” She looked away, her eyes scanning the dimly lit room as if searching for answers in the flickering shadows.

“Lucy,” Sarah implored, her voice thick with emotion. “I never meant to hurt you. You have to believe me.”

“Believe you?” Lucy's voice cracked. “How can I ever trust you again, Sarah? You knew about me and Denny. You are the only one to know about me and Denny, how he was with me, how he treated me, but yet you still…after everything, Sarah, before he went and now he’s back?”

“Please,” Sarah whispered, her eyes glistening with unshed tears. “We've been friends for so long. Can't we find a way to move past this?”

“Friends don't betray one another like this.” Lucy's words lashed out like a whip, severing the last thread of hope that bound them together. “You chose him over our friendship. You made your choice, Sarah.”

The pair fixed their eyes on each other.

"Sarah," Lucy whispered, her voice trembling with anger and sadness. "You knew how much I loved him before; you know. How could you do this to me?"

Sarah forced herself to meet her friend's eyes. "I never meant for it to happen, Lucy. It just... did. You know, he never liked you as much as you liked him."

"Did you ever stop to think about what this would do to our friendship?" Lucy demanded; her knuckles were white as she clenched her fists beneath the table. "Or was your dirty little affair all that mattered?"

"Of course not!" Sarah protested, desperation seeping into her voice. "I tried to end it, Lucy. More than once. But Denny..."

"Enough about fucking Denny!" Lucy snapped, her fury momentarily overpowering her grief. "This isn't just about him anymore, Sarah. This is about us–about everything we built together and how easily you were willing to throw it all away."

"Lucy, please," Sarah pleaded, reaching across the table in a futile attempt to bridge the widening chasm between them. "I'm so sorry."

As the reality of the situation sank in, Lucy's mind raced with a thousand unspoken questions and accusations. The betrayal she felt was like a vice around her chest, squeezing tighter until it seemed she could hardly breathe. Lucy had wanted to be with Denny, and he had turned her down. She had confided in Sarah everything about it.

"Perhaps we should just... go our separate ways," Lucy suggested quietly, though the words tasted like ash on her tongue.

"Lucy, don't say that." Sarah's eyes welled with tears, and her voice was barely audible above the murmur of the other diners. "We can work through this; I know we can."

"Can we, Sarah?" Lucy's voice broke. The anguish mirrored the pain in her eyes etched across Sarah's face.

"Peter asked me to end our business together," Sarah admitted, her voice trembling. "He's worried about us—our marriage—and he thinks we need distance from Denny and all of you, the whole gang. He thinks any links to any of you will bring us closer to him. We need a fresh start."

Sarah's eyes were brimming with tears as she finally mustered the courage to tell Lucy the genuine horrors of Denny's actions toward her.

Her hands trembled as she recounted the painful memories, and her voice shook with emotion. Her burden was almost unbearable, but she knew she needed to share it with someone she trusted. As each word spewed out, there was a sense of sorrow and betrayal. It was a difficult confession, but Sarah knew it would bring her some relief and healing.

Sarah both wanted to know that Lucy hadn't also suffered from Denny, but also wanted to know she wasn't alone. But as Lucy remained silent, a heavy weight settled in Sarah's stomach, and she knew - without words - that her worst fears had been confirmed.

Denny's actions were repulsive, a poison spreading through their heads. The betrayal sliced through her like a razor-sharp knife, leaving a searing wound that oozed with anger and pain. She could feel the cut widening, tearing her apart from the inside out as she struggled to hold back tears of rage and hurt. Knowing that both women had suffered in the same way at the hands of this man.

Lucy's nostrils flared, and her hands gripped the table's edge. The gravity of Peter's request settled in her chest, sinking like a stone.

"Distance from all of us. Is that your penalty?" Lucy's voice, sharp and accusatory. "Is that what you call it when your husband finds out about your sordid little affair?"

"Lucy, please!" Sarah pleaded, attempting to keep her voice steady. She looked around the restaurant, hoping that their conversation would remain private. "It's not like that. I didn't want to hurt you or anyone else, but Peter wants us to focus on our marriage. He thinks distancing ourselves from everyone might be best."

"Best for whom? You? Peter? And what about me, Sarah? This business is the only thing I have in my boring marriage to Graham." Lucy's anger bubbled to the surface.

"I can't ignore Peter's concerns," Sarah insisted, her chest tightening with each breath. "He knows Denny is bad news, and he doesn't want us to get caught up in his mess any longer, and that means all of you."

"Bad news, huh?" Lucy snorted, her voice dripping with sarcasm.

"And yet, you couldn't resist him, and you knew how he'd treated me," she spat, the words like venom on her tongue.

"Lucy, it's not about who he liked more. It was a mistake. I knew how he treated you, but I thought he'd be different with me. I thought he'd changed after college." Sarah whispered; her eyes downcast.

"Was it that?" Lucy challenged, her eyes narrowing as she leaned in closer to Sarah. "Or was it just another way for you to one-up me?"

"Lucy, I swear, that's not what happened," Sarah's voice cracked under her mounting guilt and sadness. "I didn't mean to hurt you."

"Of course you didn't." Lucy scoffed. "There's nothing left for me to understand. The truth is out, and there's no going back."

With a sudden surge of anger, Lucy slammed her fist onto the table, causing their wine glasses to shudder.

"You think you can just get away with this? You think I'll just let you walk away from our business and friendship without consequences?"

"Lucy, you know I would never do anything to hurt you intentionally," Sarah whispered, tears streaming down her cheeks. "I love you like a sister."

Tears rolled down Sarah's cheeks, her voice barely a whisper. "I never meant for it to end like this, Lucy."

"Neither did I," Lucy replied, her voice strained with sadness and anger. "But we can't go back now, can we?"

"Let's make this official, then," Lucy said, taking a deep breath. "We'll dissolve our partnership and go our separate ways. It's what you want, isn't it?"

Sarah hesitated for a moment, lost in thought. In her mind's eye, she saw the years of laughter and shared secrets, now overshadowed by pain and bitterness.

"Fine. We'll cut ties. It's how it has to be," Lucy said, her voice laced with finality. "But remember, Sarah, you brought this upon yourself."

A shadow of regret crossed Sarah's face, but she quickly masked it with a determined expression.

"I understand, Lucy. It's time for us both to move on."

They stood up from the table, the clatter of chairs echoing in the restaurant.

"Goodbye, Sarah," Lucy said, her voice cold and distant.

"Goodbye, Lucy," Sarah choked out, her gaze filled with sorrow and defiance.

And with that, they turned and walked away from one another, their footsteps echoing through the deserted space like the remnants of a broken trust. As they entered the night, the door closed behind them with a finality that signalled the end of an era. They turned in different directions.

"Sarah, you'll never see me again."

CHAPTER FOURTEEN

MONDAY MORNING
THE EMERALD EMPRESS
DAY THREE OF THE CRUISE

Peter, Sarah, Lucy, and Graham had hardly slept. The morning sun filtered through the sheer curtains of the breakfast room, casting a soft golden glow over the stylish decor. The room was bathed in warm cream and pale blue hues, with delicate floral patterns adorning the walls and upholstery. A large, light oak table sat in the centre, surrounded by high-backed chairs upholstered in plush velvet. The air was redolent with the rich aroma of freshly brewed coffee and the irresistible scent of pastries from the self-service buffet, which was constantly topped up by the ship's staff. It would have been the perfect breakfast if things had been different.

Sarah poured steaming cups of rich, dark coffee into delicate, floral-patterned china cups, the aroma filling the air as her hands trembled slightly, betraying her nervousness.

The group didn't need delicate china now; they needed good comforting mugs to wrap their hands around. Lucy sat at the table, her eyes darting nervously around the room, while Graham limped back and forth, his expression taut with anxiety.

"Why are you limping, Graham?" asked a genuinely concerned Peter.

"I slipped last night," Graham glanced at Lucy, who looked away.

"It hurts more if I stop moving it, so I'm trying to keep it moving; I don't think it's broken," Graham explained.

The unspoken reality was that Terri, their new friend, was now a prime suspect in Denny's murder. Fear and confusion swirled inside them as they tried to make sense of the nightmare they were living in. Each bite of food felt like lead in their stomachs as they grappled with the possibility that someone they knew could be capable of such a heinous act.

Edward Smythe walked down from the part of the ship where passengers couldn't go, his regal presence commanding attention as he entered the room; he unclipped a velvet rope, turned, and clipped it back on again as he walked through.

"Edward," said Graham, less polite than ever before. "Why on earth have you taken Terri into custody? She had nothing to do with it."

"I understand Mr Winslow, Terri Blackwood has been overheard uttering words that would make any man's blood run cold." Edward's voice carried a weight that silenced everyone. "She was heard expressing a desire for Denny's demise, her words dripping with vicious intent. Combined with the discovery of the incriminating red hoody in her room and the CCTV evidence we've uncovered, it was enough to warrant her being taken into custody, for the safety of everyone else on board. I am sorry to have to tell you this. She's very comfortable; it's not by any means a jail cell. She is completely complying with us and isn't locked in anywhere."

"I also have to tell you that, considering this tragedy, we are also returning to Southampton. Because of these stormy conditions, we will take a less open route and will go half-speed; we should be back late on Tuesday, and everyone will be refunded what they paid. Thank you."

The group dispersed like leaves scattered by an unforgiving wind, leaving them to ponder the cruel march of time that could turn friends into suspects overnight.

In the privacy of their room, Sarah paced, and Peter watched her, the rhythm of his thoughts syncing with the clock on the wall. Their sanctuary felt smaller now, compressed by the weight of unsaid words. Although the room was big for a cruise, it was still smaller than their bedroom at home.

"Sarah," Peter began, his tone gentle yet laced with an insistent undercurrent, "you knew Denny better than anyone here. Is there anything, anything at all, you're not telling me?"

She stopped pacing and turned to face him. Her direct gaze was a fortress, and her carefully chosen words were armour and sword. "Peter, I've told you everything."

"Have you though?" His suspicion, once a tiny seed, had sprouted into something more substantial, more menacing.

"You've been distant since we heard the news. I know you, Sarah. Something is on your mind."

Over the years, Peter had grown intimately acquainted with his wife's every move and gesture.

He could predict her actions before they even happened, like a dance he had practised so many times it was ingrained in his muscle memory. The slight tilt of her head and the graceful way she moved, mainly when she used the back of her hand to sweep away her hair. They all signalled something to him. Familiarity had bred an innate understanding between them that no words could ever convey. Their bond was unbreakable, forged through years of shared experiences and deeply rooted love.

A sigh escaped her lips, the sound carrying the weight of secrets held too tightly.

"I'm just... overwhelmed by all this."

"Sarah, I need to know the truth. We can't have any doubts between us, not now," Peter urged, his desire for transparency battling against his instinct to protect.

He could sense something was wrong; he wanted to believe her, oh how he wanted to.

He had married a woman of warmth and kindness, whose smiles were freely given. Yet now, as the past clawed its way into the present, he questioned the very foundation of their relationship.

Peter was the type of person who would rather just ignore things that might be upsetting or wrong.

Confrontation made his skin prickle with anxiety, so he had perfected the art of looking past discomfort, pretending not to notice the tension that crackled in the air. If a friend snapped or a stranger cast a suspicious glance his way, Peter would convince himself it was all in his imagination, a trick of his own overstimulated mind. He preferred the soft blur of denial to the sharp edges of reality. He was more intelligent than Denny or Graham, but he didn't have the confidence to use it to its full ability.

Not that he didn't care; on the contrary, Peter felt too much. The loom of what could go wrong, of what already had, pressed on him like a stone. Ignoring problems was easier, a numbing salve for the constant hum of worry. At work, when the copier broke down or deadlines spiralled into chaos, Peter would slip into the background, offering polite nods and practised smiles, avoiding the snare of responsibility. When arguments arose in his circle of friends, he would retreat into silence as if absence itself could shield him from the fallout.

The more serious the issue, the more Peter became adept at constructing walls of oblivion around himself. He thought of them as protective barriers, though deep down, he knew they were only flimsy paper defences that might one day collapse under the weight of everything left unresolved. But for now, ignorance was his refuge, a place where he could tell himself, if only for a while longer, that everything was fine.

"Alright," he agreed, though the word tasted bitter on his tongue. "But we have to stick together through this, Sarah. Whatever comes."

Sarah's fingers trembled as she clasped them tightly in her lap, the soft fabric of her sweater bunching beneath her white-knuckled grip. Peter's eyes, once a source of solace, now bore into her with an intensity that made her insides churn.

"Peter," she began, her voice barely above a whisper, "I can't let Terri suffer for what I've done." Her confession stayed between them like a fragile thread, ready to snap at the slightest touch.

"Sarah, what do you mean, 'What I've done?' What are you saying?" Peter asked, though the dread pooling in his gut told him he already knew the answer.

"I saw red, Peter. Rage. It consumed me, so I did it. I pushed him. I killed Denny. Everything was just perfect for me to end the whole thing," she confessed, her eyes glistening with tears. She was a broken woman.

"I went for a look on the deck. I wanted to see what the sea looked like in a storm. How often do you get to see that?"

Peter just looked at the floor, knowing his wife needed to tell the story.

"He stood there. I thought about everything he'd ever done to me, to any of us, and imagined how scared Terri must be.

Peter, I've never really told you what he did to me. He was already uneasy on his feet because of the drink. He looked like he was going to fall overboard on his own. I just nudged him, Pete."

Peter's world had just started falling, and he didn't know when it would stop.

"Tell me exactly what happened, Sarah." Peter pleaded.

"Ok, I will," said Sarah.

SATURDAY NIGHT
THE EMERALD EMPRESS
DAY ONE OF THE CRUISE

The salty wind whipped against her face, stinging her cheeks as she stood on the deck. Sarah's only comfort in this tumultuous storm was the fresh air, but even that was a constant struggle. The first evening of the cruise had gone ok, but she had a rage building in her that was hard to suppress. The darkness consumed her, broken only by flashes of lightning that illuminated the ship with an eerie glow. Her thoughts were a chaotic mess, like the raging sea surrounding them. With every step she took on the trembling deck, she felt the weight of Terri's troubles bearing down on her. Her memory of what Denny had done to her and all of his promises hadn't changed at all.

Then she saw him.

He was staggering around, right against the rail, looking out to sea. She knew she was a train on track, and the following moments of her life wouldn't be controllable.

"Rough night for a stroll, isn't it, Denny?" said Sarah, knowing she was staring at a sequence of events that wouldn't stop.

"Why are you here?" Denny demanded, peering into the gloom.

"Terri, is that you? I told you I'll be back down shortly; tell me why you're here, and stop bloody raining!" demanded Denny, looking to the skies.

"Your authority doesn't extend to the weather or me," Sarah replied, annoyed that the great Denny thought he could haul this storm or anything Sarah could do.

"Is this some kind of joke?" Denny snapped, squaring his shoulders, ready to confront the bold intruder. "I'm in no mood for games."

"I'm not in the mood for games either," Sarah said, stepping into the dim glow of an emergency light. Lightning cracked overhead, but she knew that the hood of her beige overcoat would mask her face.

"Then why lurk in the dark? Speak your piece, Terri." Denny growled, his tone betraying his eagerness to exert control over the situation.

"Oh, I have nothing to say," said Sarah.

She pulled back her hood to reveal her face to Denny.

A flash of recognition passed across his face, almost comforted that he knew the person facing him.

Denny's reflexes were sluggish, his body unprepared for the assault.

Sarah knew she had one attempt at pushing Denny overboard to negate a struggle. She was also conscious that she didn't want to go over with him, so as a precaution, she had looped a rope from the deck onto her arm, not knowing how much safety it actually provided.

With a violent shove, Denny felt his feet slip beneath him, his balance vanishing as quickly as his hopes of overpowering Sarah. His back hit the railing with a sickening thud, the metal cold and unyielding against his spine. Water surged below, a maelstrom waiting with open jaws.

Sarah watched as Denny's body hit the icy water, and his splash quickly disappeared into the darkness along the ship's side.

Sarah stood alone, watching the spot where Denny had disappeared. No words were spoken; none were needed. The deed was done, and the sea would keep its secrets.

Sarah stood there to ensure that Denny did not reappear above the surface and that none of his cries were heard.

Whether the impact on the sea killed Denny or the cold of the North Sea, Denny was dead.

MONDAY MORNING
THE EMERALD EMPRESS
DAY THREE OF THE CRUISE

"So, that's what happened," said Sarah, shaking uncontrollably.

"Thank you for telling me that, but Sarah, we must think this through," Peter urged, struggling to keep his voice steady as he grappled with the enormity of his wife's revelation. His mind raced, torn between the law he respected and his love for the woman before him. He reached for her hand, the familiar warmth a balm to the icy fear that threatened to overtake them both. "Say nothing. For now. I just can't think this through on the spot." Said Peter with his face in his hands.

"But Peter, the red hoody, I wasn't wearing it. It was nothing to do with me."

Sarah felt sick as she again paced the confines of their suite, each step a measure of time slipping through her fingers. She would do anything to turn back the clock. Peter watched her from his perch on the edge of the bed, his eyes tracing the lines of worry etched into her face.

“Peter,” she said, halting mid-pace, “they haven't found me on the CCTV footage.” Her voice quivered with a mixture of fear and perplexity. “There has to be a reason. A technical glitch, perhaps? Or maybe... maybe the cameras missed me somehow? But they said they'd seen Denny on deck.”

Peter remained silent for a moment, considering her words.

“It's possible; there are a few ways out onto that deck, right? I want to go and check, but that would look weird,” he finally replied, his tone measured. “The ship is enormous, and the network might have blind spots. Didn't Smythe say that? But you're right. The ship's security said they'd seen him go out on deck. But, if they'd have seen you, they'd have asked you.” Peter's words were now rambling as his mouth couldn't keep up with his thoughts.

Sarah clasped her hands tightly, trying to still their trembling. The thought of being caught was unbearable. She had been so careful and precise all her life, yet now she felt as if she were standing on the precipice of a great chasm, the ground beneath her eroding with every passing second. The fact that Terri was under suspicion was eating into her.

“I’m so scared,” she murmured, more to herself than to Peter.

Sarah's mind raced back to arriving on the Emerald Empress less than 48 hours ago; although things seemed unbearable, she had no idea those were the good times, and these were the bad. She longed for the simplicity of those times, the comfort of believing that the world was a place where justice prevailed.

Sarah couldn't even start coming to terms with the fact of whether or not she was caught. She was still a murderer. No matter how awful Denny was, she was a murderer.

As they sat entwined in their cocoon of dread, a knock at the door shattered their fragile sanctuary. Peter rose to answer it. Standing in the doorway was Graham, his face a mask of bewilderment and disbelief.

“The security team has just confirmed something,” Graham announced, his voice cutting through the tense atmosphere. “Terri... she was seen on the CCTV footage at the time of Denny's disappearance. She was on a different deck, way above Denny. She couldn’t have got down there in time; she didn’t do it.”

A collective gasp rippled through the air as Sarah's mind grappled with the implications. Terri, the woman who had endured their suspicions, was innocent—at least, in the eyes of the omnipresent cameras.

"She wasn't wearing the red hoody either," Graham continued, the words tumbling out as if he were struggling to make sense of the revelation. "It was a mistake, a terrible mistake. Several passengers have reported someone moving around the ship in that red hoody, but it wasn't Terri."

In the wake of this news, the room seemed to spin around Sarah, the walls closing in as she fought to maintain her composure. This unexpected twist of fate both relieved and terrified her. If they knew Terri was not the killer, then suspicion would inevitably turn elsewhere, and the tenuous thread that held her secret could unravel with the slightest tug. Or would people conclude that he'd been there alone, and that it was an accident? How could they have footage to prove Terri's innocence but not to prove Sarah's guilt?

"Thank you, Graham," Peter said, his voice steady despite the turmoil brewing within him. He closed the door gently, turning back to Sarah with a look of deep concern.

"Sarah, what are we going to do?" he asked, his eyes searching hers for an answer neither of them had.

She sank onto the bed beside him. The past was a relentless pursuer, its shadows stretching out to touch the present. The truth of what she had done threatening to emerge and engulf them all.

"We wait; I just wanted to get off this ship," she whispered, her gaze fixed on the undulating waves outside the porthole. "We wait and hope we get off this ship on Wednesday."

The seconds ticked by, each one a reminder of the uncertainty that lay ahead, a future fraught with the spectres of regret and recrimination. Sarah knew that time was a fickle friend.

CHAPTER FIFTEEN

MONDAY EVENING

THE EMERALD EMPRESS

DAY 3 OF THE CRUISE

As the sun set and the shadows lengthened, the friends who had spent the day in their respective rooms gathered at their usual spot for their evening, still processing the last few days, trying to act as normal as they could muster. They weren't here to mingle with strangers or attend a party, but simply for the safety of known faces and to not be driven mad by the same four walls. Despite the noise of the surrounding crowd, their table felt like its own little world, a safe haven where they could let down their guard and just be themselves. As they sipped their drinks, time seemed to slow down, allowing them to savour this precious moment together.

Terri Blackwood stepped back into the circle of friends; it was awkward. Her release from custody lifted a weight from their collective shoulders while simultaneously anchoring a heavy stone of doubt.

"Good to have you back," Lucy offered, her voice tentative, as if unsure whether the words would bridge or widen the gap that had formed.

Each member greeted Terri with a warm, genuine hug.

"Thanks," Terri replied, her eyes scanning the faces around her for signs of trust or betrayal. Each friend seemed to be an island unto themselves, separated by currents of unease that flowed between them, invisible yet palpable.

Sarah watched from a distance, her heart racing. Her facade was a thin veneer, threatening to crack under the burden of her hidden truth. Guilt clawed at her insides, each beat of her heart a reminder of the life she had taken and the innocence she now stole with every breath.

Sarah flashed memories of Denny's cruel smirk, the way he lorded over everyone with his evil charm. Her hand trembled at her side. The secret she harboured was a spectre that threatened to rise from the depths at any moment.

As they convened around a table laden with untouched snacks and tepid drinks, the group struggled to rekindle the warmth that had once defined them. Even the ship's waiting staff had abandoned them; it seemed they didn't pay the group the same attention they had. Lucy looked at a gin and tonic on the table that she hadn't touched for 20 minutes. On the first night, someone would have asked if she'd like a fresh one or at least if this discarded one would be taken away.

"Well, at least we don't have much time left on this bloody boat," Peter said, his attempt at normalcy sounding strained. His eyes met Sarah's, a silent conversation passing between them.

Sarah nodded, her smile brittle.

She imagined drifting towards the railing in quieter moments, peering into the churning sea below. The past collided with the present, the echo of Denny's last gasp swallowed by the waves. She pondered the passage of time, how it could erase evidence but not the stain of remorse. She wondered what Denny thought before his last breath when he gave up fighting against the waves. How did the icy water feel when it hit him? Was he too drunk to feel it? Did he, in his last moments, understand why he did it?

"Are you alright?" Graham's voice broke through her dream, his concern genuine but tinged with the residue of doubt that clung to them all.

"Fine," Sarah lied, her response automatic as the past folded into the present again. The ship slid forward through the night, towards home, its course steady, while beneath its gleaming surface, the gears of fate continued to grind, shaping a future where the past refused to stay buried.

The sun dipped beneath the horizon, casting a crimson glow across the deck outside. The group huddled inside around a table strewn with cocktail napkins and drained dirty glasses, safe from the still-raging storm.

Sarah felt the weight of their stares. Although she knew they were probably not looking at her more than before, she felt it more.

"Accidents happen," she mumbled, almost to herself, the lie tasting bitter on her tongue. "Maybe we'll never really know what happened."

As the evening wore on, she couldn't get the thought of the ship's CCTV system out of her head. Why hadn't they found her yet? Indeed, the cameras had been watching, unblinking eyes recording every move.

The Emerald Empress was the height of innovative technology; how could it have a partially working CCTV system?

Later, the darkness enveloped her in her room. It crept in from the corners, the edges of the walls seeming to breathe as if the ship itself held its breath, waiting. She sat on the bed, knees pulled to her chest, eyes wide and unblinking, tracing the shapes that moved just beyond the lamplight. Her secret whispered to her in a voice that was both familiar and unknown, a twisted echo of her own thoughts.

At first, she tried to dismiss it as exhaustion. But the whispers grew bolder, speaking in fragmented phrases, half-formed words that slithered into her mind like worms burrowing deep. She pressed her hands to her ears, but it was useless; the voice came from within, wrapping around her thoughts until they were indistinguishable from the taunts.

As the minutes stretched into night, reality fractured. The room seemed to warp; the furniture taking on crooked, hunched shapes as if mocking her from the dark. She would turn to catch a glimpse of movement, a shadow that didn't belong to her, only for it to vanish when she blinked.

The mirror across the room became a thing of dread, reflecting not her own face but a version of it twisted by a cruel, knowing smile. A murderer.

She tried to reason with herself and bring logic to the chaos, but the lines between her thoughts and the voice's taunts began to blur. "They'll know soon," it would hiss, sharp and venomous.

"They'll see what you've done."

It was silent now.

But in that silence, she felt a presence inching closer. The last tether of her sanity snapped as she watched a hand, thin and pale as bone, reach out from the dark.

Sarah's thoughts danced erratically, flitting from the warmth of Peter's embrace to the cold finality of Denny's absence. The ship was now possibly passing near to where Denny's body would be in the water. But Sarah dismissed these thoughts.

A sudden gust of wind rattled the balcony door, and she flinched, a jolt of adrenaline surging through her veins. It was as if the universe itself was conspiring to startle her into confession, tearing away the veil of composure she clung to so desperately.

The storm outside continued to rage, but she had blanked it out from her consciousness.

She wouldn't care if the whole ship went down with everyone on it; it would be a way out. Thunder boomed and lightning flashed, casting brief moments of eerie brightness into the dark room. Rain pounded against the windows, creating a symphony of drumming sounds that echoed through the house. The wind howled like an animal in pain, rattling the windows and shaking the walls.

"Denny! Leave me!" Sarah uncontrollably.

For a fleeting instant, Sarah's eyes widened as she glanced out of the window and caught a glimpse of a figure on the balcony, backlit by a sudden burst of lightning. Only the edges of the figure illuminated. The figure appeared to be drenched and shimmering in the eerie glow. She blinked, and the figure was gone. With a start, Sarah realised she must have been dozing off and conjured the image in her half-awake state. Rain tapping against the window lulled her into a peaceful sleep, her mind wandering into the realm of dreams.

In that unforgettable moment, she knew with a deep ache that Denny would linger in her thoughts for years to come. His image would haunt her dreams, and his voice would echo in the empty spaces of her mind; every time she slipped into a dream, he would be there.

Memories of him would flood her senses at unexpected times, causing her heart to tighten and tears to well up in her eyes. Yes, Denny would stay with her, a bittersweet ghost that she couldn't escape from.

"Peter," she whispered, her voice barely carrying across the room, "Why can't they see me?"

But the question remained unanswered, swallowed by the vast silence that enveloped them. Sarah rose and approached the window.

Sarah's mind drifted back to the day she met him, the way his smile seemed like a promise of something beautiful but turned into a nightmare. But promises, she now knew, were fragile things—easily made and easily broken.

She sat on the bed, eyes wide and unblinking, tracing the shapes that moved just beyond the lamplight. She had decided that she couldn't sleep, so she would admit defeat and do something else.

At that moment, a noise came from the hallway, right outside her door. The sound, almost imperceptible, was enough to make her jump.

"Who's there?" Her voice cracked, the edges of panic fraying.

No response came, and for a fleeting moment, Sarah wondered if she had imagined it—the product of a mind teetering on the brink of madness. Then, a slip of paper slid under the door, silent as a whisper, yet screaming with implication. She approached it as one might approach a viper, knowing the sting it could deliver. With trembling hands, she picked up the note and unfolded it, her eyes scanning the words scrawled in haste:

"We need to talk about the night Denny died. I know you were there. I know you did it, but I understand. We can work this out."

The note was written on the paper that was supplied in each room, a drawing and the words 'THE EMERALD EMPRESS' across the top.

There was nothing else on the paper, and there were no instructions.

Sarah found it hard to catch her breath. She didn't want Peter to wake up and hadn't decided whether to mention the note.

What would happen now? Who penned the message that threatened to unravel her life?

Sarah decided no instructions meant she needed to leave now. She grabbed her coat, put on some jogging bottoms, and opened the door, glancing back at Peter sleeping on the bed. She needed to confront whoever this was alone.

CHAPTER SIXTEEN

TUESDAY MORNING, EARLY HOURS
THE EMERALD EMPRESS
DAY FOUR OF THE CRUISE

The corridor was empty, starkly contrasting with the cacophony of late-night laughter reverberating from the distant ballroom. Sarah's fingers brushed against the fabric of her coat, the soft wool a shield against the chill that seemed to seep from the Emerald Empress's steel bones. She had just clicked her door shut; the sound echoing in the hollowness. In the corner of her eye, she saw a figure standing in the darkness at the end of the hall.

Edward Smythe stood there, an immovable fixture, his tall frame casting a long shadow under the dim lighting. The silver threads in his hair caught the light like whispers of moonlight, a reminder of the passage of time that turned people into enigmas. Although his face was in darkness, his eyes were visible. His presence carried a gravity that made the air around him feel denser.

"Mrs. Emerson," he greeted.

"Mr. Smythe," Sarah replied, her voice steady despite the sudden tightness gripping her chest. She watched his eyes, those sharp blue pools that held stories untold, as they fixed on her with an intensity that hinted at urgency.

"May I have a word? In private?" Edward's request wasn't really a question, laced with an importance that couldn't be ignored. He stepped aside, gesturing toward the direction of his quarters with a hand that suggested both a command and an invitation.

Sarah hesitated, aware of the tendrils of doubt trying to cloud her judgment. Yet, the pull of secrecy and intrigue tugged at her curiosity. There was no way she wouldn't talk to him. He had written the note; he knew everything.

"Of course," she assented; her steps measured as she followed Edward down the hallway.

Their footsteps were the only sound, a rhythm against the plush carpet that led them away from prying eyes. The walls adorned with framed glimpses of the cruise liner's prestigious history watching over them, silent guardians of the present shaped by the deeds of the past.

Inside Edward's quarters, there was a stark contrast to the ornate hallway. Modern, with clean lines and minimal decorations, the space reflected Edward's penchant for control and order. He had obviously asked for it to be decorated differently than the rest of the ship. Sarah's gaze fell upon a large screen that dominated one wall, its surface as dark and still as a moonless night sea and it looked out of place in these surroundings.

"Please, have a seat," Edward gestured toward a sleek chair opposite his desk.

Sarah complied, her coat whispering against the back of the chair as she settled in. She folded her hands in her lap, attempting to project calmness, but her heart betrayed her, pounding relentlessly.

Edward took his time seating himself behind the desk, the weight of his gaze fixed on Sarah. He reached into a drawer and produced a remote control; it clicked as he turned on the screen, buzzing ominously in the quiet room.

The display flickered to life and Sarah's breath caught in her throat as she witnessed CCTV footage of herself on the deck, the wind playing with loose strands of her hair — and there was Denny, unaware of the storm approaching him from behind.

"Sarah," Edward's voice cut through the shock that had wrapped itself around her. "This is the moment you pushed Denny overboard."

Sarah glanced at the screen and saw herself approaching Denny.

"But, let's not put you through that," said Edward, clicking pause on the remote control, leaving a still on the screen of Sarah with her hands on Denny's chest.

At that moment, Sarah knew everything was about to change. Edward knew everything that had happened.

Her eyes darted to Edward's face, searching for a sign of mercy or malice. But his expression remained unreadable, a mask carved from years of business gambits and silent power struggles.

"Nobody else has seen this footage," Edward continued, his tone even, almost dispassionate. "I've made certain of that. This is the only copy of it in the world."

"Wh-why?" Sarah's voice was barely a whisper. The chill of fear drained away her usual warmth.

"Control, Sarah, and you have confused my original plan," Edward said, leaning back in his chair, the leather creaking softly under his weight.

"I control everything on this ship. What is seen, what is heard, and what remains hidden. My security team is useless on purpose."

He paused, letting his words hang in the air, heavy with implication. "The security team thinks they know what happened to Denny. They believe he simply... vanished, fell over, jumped over. A drunk person falling overboard that's easier, much less paperwork for them. But I know the truth, and now, you know that I also know the truth."

Sarah felt the walls closing in, the room suddenly too small, Edward's power too vast. The past, something she thought she could bury at sea, had resurfaced with a vengeance.

"Please," she started, her plea cut short by the raising of Edward's hand.

"Save your breath," he said. "We have much to discuss and little time."

In those words, Sarah understood that her fate was no longer her own. She was bound to this man by the weight of her actions, her secret tethered to his will.

The room was still as if the air waited for Edward's following words. What could he possibly want from her? Sarah sat rigidly.

The faint scent of aged mahogany, mixed with the brine of the sea outside, reminded her of the vastness that surrounded them and the isolation it imposed.

"Your actions were... unforeseen," Edward began, his eyes fixed on Sarah with unsettling intensity. "You see, Sarah, someone was supposed to fall off the ship on this trip, but it wasn't Denny. This whole thing was leading to our friend Graham having a little slip on the deck, never to be seen again."

"What? Graham?! But you're friends?" replied Sarah.

Sarah's breath hitched, her mind racing. Graham, their pleasant companion, the man who had laughed with them at dinner just hours before? What had he done to earn Edward's disdain?

Edward rose from his chair. "Graham's restaurant crippled my family's business, reduced them to nothing, breaking my family apart."

I gave him a tremendous opportunity to do the menus for this ship, but he used it against me.

Sarah sat there silently, knowing Edward was about to expand.

“His restaurant, the only one he opened,” Edward continued, his voice tinged with a mixture of bitterness and resolve, “was not just a simple business venture. It was strategically placed near my parents' establishment, siphoning off their loyal customers.”

Sarah's eyes widened in realisation as the pieces fell into place.

“My parents,” Edward said in a low growl.

“They watched helplessly as Graham's deceitful charm lured away their loyal customers. Their once-thriving authentic restaurant became a mere shadow of its former self, struggling to stay afloat after Graham's departure. Worst of all, he did it all on purpose.”

Sarah felt a surge of empathy for Edward, recognising the pain and betrayal he must have felt witnessing the downfall of his family's legacy.

“They were the most important people in the world to me, Sarah. I even introduced Graham to them around the time he did the menus for this ship. My father even said to him that the area was prime for a restaurant of his kind, never expecting he would do that. My father was good to him. I was good to him. “

Sarah looked at the floor. It was clear that Edward was genuinely upset.

"He opened his restaurant right across the street; my father kept it from me for the whole time. I could have helped them with money. But he was too proud. I'd just bought this ship. I had borrowed a lot of money, and I'm sure he didn't want to spoil anything for me. Their restaurant customers dried up; he used all his savings, and then…."

"What?" said Sarah.

"He ended things. He killed himself. He couldn't face the failure. He couldn't face his future. He didn't even tell my mother what was going on." Edward's voice quivered.

"Oh, Edward, I'm sorry."

"If Dad would have just given us a chance to help him. If I could turn back time, he'd still be here."

"You know what, Sarah? Graham went around to their restaurant one day when he first opened it, asking them if they had any fresh thyme. My mother went and cut some from their garden for him and gave it to him."

Edward's stance shifted from a beaten man to someone seeking revenge.

"So, that's why things have to end for him, Sarah," Edward said in a determined voice.

"But Edward, as someone who let their rage get the better of them, I regret it now. I'll regret it forever. Denny was a monster. I've never talked to anyone about what happened between him and me, but if I told you everything, you'd know why I did it. But Graham? He's not a bad person. You were going to kill someone for being a shrewd businessman?"

"No, I'm going to kill him for taking my father away." Edward momentarily lost his composure and shouted these words in the silent room.

Sarah nodded knowingly.

"So, Sarah, I decided this is what I wanted to do. I called him a few months back, offering him some rooms. I knew I had to offer some for his friends, too. It would look too odd, just inviting him and Lucy. I knew you all had…" Edward chose his words carefully.

"…some history." Edward smiled a crazed smile.

He continued, "I knew Graham wouldn't pass up that offer, even if it were out of the blue and completely out of context for our friendship; I knew his ego would get the better of him. I just needed to get him here."

"So, this now calls for a different plan," Edward smirked.

"Ok, so what's the deal?" Sarah wanted to sound business-like.

Edward reached to the TV and pulled out a small hard drive which had been plugged into the back.

"Sarah, this is the only copy of the footage that proves you pushed Denny. Help me kill Graham, and I'll never, ever show this to anyone. If you help me, we'll throw it overboard, along with our other secrets. Believe me, I have a plan that will make you appear completely innocent; you just have to help me."

"How can I trust you won't keep a copy? I could help you, and you could show everyone afterwards?" said Sarah.

"What would my motive be? I don't want to get you into trouble, Sarah. I understand why you killed Denny. Even though you won't share the extent of how he treated you, I know it must have been bad. But because things have changed, I now need your help. Graham will be much more suspicious after what's happened to Denny. I have no reason to show it to anyone."

The room seemed to sway, reality blurring at the edges. Sarah thought of her friends, of the trust they placed in her, and of the bonds they shared.

How could she betray them? Yet, what choice did she have when Edward held the key to her future?

"Time is of the essence," Edward pressed on.

"We must act swiftly and decisively. This boat will be back in Southampton in 48 hours. I've ordered the captain to sail back slowly, saying that I want to make the passengers feel safe in this storm but really to give myself more time."

She nodded, her response automatic, the words lodged in her throat.

With a final nod of acquiescence, Sarah sealed her fate.

She would play her part in Edward's vendetta; her history is a chain that bound her to his cause.

Sarah was motionless, the silence in Edward's quarters stretching taut like a wire. The revelation of his vendetta against her friend Graham seemed to reverberate off the opulent walls, each word a hammer strike against her conscience. Graham meant more to Sarah than anyone knew, but now she faced a dilemma: choosing between him and her freedom.

"Edward, I..." Her voice faltered, the words dissolving into the air.

"Sarah, my dear," Edward began, his tone smooth as silk yet edged with steel, "we both know that this is not a matter of choice for you."

She felt the weight of his gaze, those sharp blue eyes that seemed to strip away her defences, leaving her exposed—the warmth of her nurturing smile lost to the chill of fear. She thought of Denny, his cruel laughter now a ghostly echo in her memory, and how one impulsive act had entangled her in this web of deceit.

"Your friends need not be involved," Edward continued, his hands clasped behind his back as he paced slowly before her. "This is between you, me, and Graham. Your... indiscretion remains our secret, so long as you cooperate."

"Understand, Sarah, I am not without sympathy for your predicament," Edward said, pausing to stand before her. "But I must protect what is mine. And you, unfortunately, are now part of that protection."

"Very well," she whispered, each syllable a stone in her stomach. "What's the plan?"

"Good." Edward's voice was devoid of triumph, merely the acknowledgement of a transaction completed. "Remember, discretion is paramount. We cannot afford slip-ups. Oh, excuse the pun."

Sarah couldn't believe he was making a joke at a time like this.

As Sarah turned to leave, the moment's gravity pressed down upon her. The ornate clock on the mantle ticked away, indifferent to the history within these walls.

Sarah felt like a marionette, strings pulled by Edward's knowing hands.

"Let me detail things," Edward began, his words slicing through the fog of Sarah's thoughts.

"You just have to get Graham alone on the deck tomorrow night. On our way home, we will be in the right position—nowhere near any ports or other boats, ironically, in the same position where Denny met his end on the way out." Edward chuckled. "At least the friends will be reunited."

"I need you to get him on deck and somehow get his phone. I will make sure he goes overboard. You leave his phone on the bench on the deck for me to pick up. It would be best if you didn't have to watch it. So, get him to deck, get his phone, put it on the bench, and get away."

"Ok," said Sarah. "I have no choice."

"You don't," said Edward. "But imagine getting off this ship knowing what happened to Denny will stay secret forever.

I know that my secret is safe with you, too; you'll never be able to prove I had anything to do with Graham's murder. I control all the CCTV on this ship before my useless security gets anywhere near it. The cameras that recorded you have today been removed, so I don't have to worry about any footage of me doing the same thing."

Sarah stared into space.

"So, Sarah, to recap, get him to deck, get his phone. That's it."

"Ok, but what time?" said Sarah.

"It doesn't matter. After dark, I'll be watching you and tracking you; I am all the time." Edward smirked.

The gravity of the act clawed at Sarah's resolve. Betraying a friend seemed wrong to her very being, yet the echo of her past loomed more significant than any bond of friendship. Denny's face flashed in her mind's eye, cruel and taunting, a reminder of the woman she once was—a woman capable of rage, of violence.

Sarah's breath caught. Could she live with the stain of another's demise on her conscience? Could she endure the whispers of betrayal that would haunt her dreams? Her friend Lucy would be a widow. She wouldn't be the hand that made it happen, but she would be an accessory.

"Remember, Sarah," Edward said, his voice an indistinct murmur echoing from a distant past, "glorious moments are born from great opportunity. And that's what you have here tonight."

"Remember, discretion is paramount," Edward cautioned, standing to escort her to the door. His voice was the rustle of silk against steel, smooth but unyielding.

"We won't talk again until it's done," Edward said, but if you don't get him to deck tomorrow night, I give the footage over to the authorities as soon as they board the ship, which we've been informed they will, as soon as they can.

Sarah felt the chill of the corridor seep through her coat as she stepped out of the warmth of Edward's lair. She turned back to him, her eyes searching his for some semblance of humanity, but she found none. He was a master sculptor; she was merely clay in his hands.

"Until tomorrow then," he said, the finality of his tone suggesting that their conversation—and her fate—was sealed.

As the door closed behind her with a soft click, Sarah's legs moved mechanically, carrying her away from the epicentre of deception.

She had crossed a line, the memory of Denny's fall now mirrored by the looming event of Graham's untimely end.

The ship cut through the night, indifferent to the fates it carried. Sarah pressed a hand against the cool glass, the barrier between her and the abyss. Her reflection stared back, a stranger cloaked in the guise of the woman she once knew.

"Forgive me," she murmured, though she knew absolution was out of reach now.

CHAPTER SEVENTEEN

TUESDAY MORNING

THE EMERALD EMPRESS

DAY FOUR OF THE CRUISE

The morning light crept through the blinds. Peter lay awake, his stocky frame rigid beneath the sheets. Beside him, Sarah's hair fanned out on her pillow, her breaths deep and even. His eyes, usually warm with laughter, now darted anxiously around the room as though seeking an escape from his thoughts.

"Sarah," he whispered, his voice hoarse with a night's unspoken confessions.

She stirred, blinking away the remnants of dreams. "Peter? What's wrong?"

"I can't... stop thinking about what you did," he said.

Sarah's face tightened, the burden in her eyes reflecting her internal struggle. "I know," she hissed. "But we can't change it now."

"Can't we?" Peter's question was less about possibility and more an echo of his turmoil. He wanted to believe in absolution, but the image of Denny, cold and lifeless, haunted him.

As they dressed in silence, the tension was palpable. The familiar clang of cutlery and the murmur of conversation served as the backdrop for their breakfast. They had sat at the same table every morning and now it started to feel familiar. Terri, Peter, Graham, Lucy and Sarah gathered around the table. Plates were passed mechanically and toast and coffee were consumed without taste. They were eating because they knew they needed to.

This was not the breakfast anyone imagined they would be having. They thought these breakfasts would be happy, even if they were forced.

"Where do we stand with the search?" asked Terri, her sharp tone slicing through the uneasy quiet. The ship's crew had kept her updated, but she wanted to hear from them.

"It remains at a standstill," replied Graham, his eyes flitting from face to face, searching for a crack in their collective facade.

"They can't send out a search from the mainland; we're still too far and the storm is too heavy," he glanced at Lucy, "and the recovery of.... something from the water would be too dangerous."

Lucy stood up, threw her napkin at the table and stormed off.

"Lucy!" Sarah cried out, but her friend didn't turn back.

"Someone here knows more than they're letting on," Terri pressed, her gaze lingering on Graham.

"Are you still suggesting one of us is involved?" Graham's voice rose defensively, her fork clattering against his plate.

"Isn't that obvious?" Terri shot back. "Denny had enemies, but who here had the opportunity? You weren't exactly friends, Graham."

Peter felt Sarah stiffen beside him, her carefully chosen words poised on the edge of her lips. "We were all on the boat that night," she countered, her direct gaze challenging the group. "Any one of you could be accused. You have no apology to make to me. If you had anything to do with it, tell me." Terri challenged the group.

"I'm glad he's dead."

"Accusations should have evidence," Peter interjected, trying to sound reasonable despite his guilty knowledge.

"Maybe we should just let the security team handle this," suggested Sarah, her attempt at peace-making feeble against the rising tide of distrust.

"Because they've been so helpful so far? I wonder how many qualifications you need to be security on a cruise ship?" Terri's sarcasm was a bitter pill no one wanted to swallow.

"Let's not turn on each other," Sarah said, her voice quivering but a beacon of calm in the storm. "Denny was so drunk that night he went outside during a storm on a slimy deck. He would have been leaning over and slipped."

Sarah's fingers curled around the warm ceramic of her coffee mug. She took a sip, allowing the bitter liquid to scald her tongue, a penance for the deceit that soured her thoughts.

"Something on your mind?" Graham asked, his voice gentle yet probing.

"Nothing more than usual," she lied. Sarah knew her betrayal of Graham was a splinter wedged deep within her, decaying with each passing moment and having breakfast with the man that she had agreed to kill. She was trying to hate him.

Knowing he only had 12 hours to live was a feeling she couldn't understand or contemplate the weight of, but she had no choice; she had to go along with it.

The others started to leave the breakfast room, leaving without saying goodbye. Sarah and Peter sat there.

"Are you ready?" he said.

"I'm going to get some more juice; you go back."

He smiled, knowing instinctively that she needed some space.

As she got up to leave, she looked down at the table and saw the knife. Small but sharp, used for cutting a solid block of butter on the table, it could almost fit in someone's palm. Without thinking it through, she put the knife in her pocket. She had no plan, but she knew that deviating from Edward's plan would mean something drastic, and whatever it was, she knew she would probably need a knife.

Hours passed, with the couples confined in their rooms. This was the most time the group hadn't seen each other. No contact, no pleasantries. Sarah sat in her room, staring out the window at the storm, which had settled a little for now, with the first glimpse of the sun for days.

An eerie light landed and the waves now looked beautiful, transporting Sarah to a place where she could think through the problem. There was a way out of this for her, for Peter and she knew doing anything to save Graham would sacrifice herself.

Later that evening, she watched Peter, the man who knew her darkest secrets yet chose to cradle them like delicate glassware. He didn't know about the secret agreement with Edward. He didn't know the closest person to him in the world was about to double her crime.

"I'm heading to the gym," he said, his eyes avoiding hers as if even a glance might shatter the precarious equilibrium they'd constructed.

"I need just to do something normal,"

Peter didn't ever go to the gym, but Sarah couldn't bring herself to joke about that. When he packed his gym clothes, neither of them actually expected him to use them; the lure of food and drink would always have won.

"Of course," she murmured.

She couldn't believe he could go to the gym at a time like this, but she also knew he always was someone who needed to take his mind off things, avoiding them rather than confronting them.

Peter paused at the door. Sarah could feel the look from across the room. Their shared silence spoke volumes, doubt and loyalty entwined in that brief hesitation.

"Peter," she began, but the words lodged in her throat.

He offered a weak smile. "It's okay, Sarah. We'll figure this out." With that, he was gone, leaving her alone with the ghosts of her guilt.

Sarah's gaze lingered on the closed door, her mind a whirlwind of what-ifs and should-haves. She had chosen this path, a treacherous road paved with good intentions and desperate measures. But where did it lead?

The clock ticked on, indifferent to her need to think. Each second reminded her that time was slipping through her fingers and, with it, the chance to set things right. She had to act to confront things head-on. She knew she couldn't help to kill Graham, but she also knew she was trapped.

Rising from the chair, Sarah steadied herself, her resolve hardening like steel. Tonight, she would face Graham, come what may. The truth was a blade poised at her neck, and only by grasping it firmly could she hope to wield it without cutting herself.

She hadn’t even thought about how to get Graham to the deck if she had to. Would she be safe if she turned up alone and Edward was there? Could she reason with Edward once more?

The knock on her door was soft, but insistent. Sarah's heartbeat quickened as she crossed the room, assuming Peter had forgotten something. She opened the door to find Graham standing there, the impeccable lines of his tailored suit. He looked desperate.

“May I come in?” His voice was a low murmur, a subtle plea that tugged at something deep within her.

“Of course,” she replied, stepping aside. As he entered, she noticed his eyes didn’t quite meet hers, as if he were building up to something.

Graham took a deep breath, his fingers brushing through his perfectly styled hair—a rare gesture of unease. “Sarah, I can't keep this to myself any longer,” he began, his eloquence faltering momentarily. “I feel suffocated in my marriage. Lucy and I are like two strangers living under the same roof. We haven’t slept in the same room for years. You’re one of my closest friends; I needed to tell someone. I can’t do it anymore. I’m a shell of a man.”

Of all the things Sarah thought Graham might blurt out, this wasn't it. Even though Sarah was taking it in, she couldn't help looking at him, thinking that she could be looking at someone in the last hours of their life; that was a strange feeling, but something with momentum that she felt she couldn't stop. Sarah wondered whether there would be a point in the future where she would wish she could return to this moment and change things. It was then she knew she had to change the plan.

"Marriages go through rough patches," Sarah said, her words measured, but her voice betrayed a hint of empathy.

"Rough patch?" He scoffed lightly, the mischievous glint in his eye dulled by sadness. "It's been a Cold War for years. But you," he paused, taking a tentative step closer.

"With you, I feel alive. You see me, Sarah—not the facade, but the real me. You always have. Since college. I've been building up to say this to you when we booked this cruise; I've been planning this conversation for months."

Sarah's throat tightened. The intensity in his gaze unsettled her, stirring a dangerous longing.

She struggled to maintain her composure as her desires clawed at her resolve.
"Please, don't," she whispered, averting her gaze. "Please don't. We've been here before and done this a few times."
"I have to. Because..." Graham hesitated, searching her face for anything that might mirror his confession. "Because I…. care for you deeply."
Sarah knew he had aborted his use of the word love.
"I have cared for you for as long as I can remember," Graham's voice quivered with raw emotion.
"Since we were children, playing by the river before I met Lucy."
Sarah's eyes widened at his revelation, her heart thudding in her chest as memories of their shared past flooded her mind. She recalled the innocence of their youth, the laughter that echoed through sunlit afternoons and the unspoken bond that had always tethered them together.
She had never dared entertain the possibility that Graham harboured feelings for her beyond friendship. He had said it once, but never during the constraints of their respective marriages.

There had always been a spark between them, and there were times in their past when it could have happened.

“Graham...” Sarah's voice faltered, “I feel something for you. I always have. I need to tell you that.”

There it was, the raw truth laid bare between them, as tangible as the charged air that preceded the storm. Yet Sarah felt herself teetering on the edge of an abyss, torn between the warmth of his affection and the chilling knowledge of what lay ahead. How could she reconcile these feelings when his life was ticking away, closer than he knew? At that moment, she finally admitted to herself that she had always liked Graham and had to do something.

“Graham, this isn't right,” she said, her voice more robust now, though it did little to mask the quiver of conflict within. “You're married, and things... they're complicated.”

“Complicated can be exhilarating,” he countered, a desperate edge creeping into his voice.

“Don't you feel it, too? This connection?”

She did; oh, how she did. But admitting it would only entwine their fates further, binding her to a truth she wasn't sure she dared to face.

And yet, denying it would be a lie that tasted like deceit on her tongue.

"It's a terrible idea," Sarah managed to say, her heart aching with the weight of secrets.

"Especially now."

"Is it because of Denny?" Graham asked, his intuition slicing through the layers of her defences.

"Everything is because of Denny," she admitted, evoking a shadow that still loomed over them.

"Then let's forget the world for a moment," he urged, closing the distance between them.

"Let's just be Graham and Sarah—two people who found a light in the dark."

But Sarah knew better. With every word, every look, she risked being consumed by the fire of their connection—one that threatened to engulf them both.

"I need to think, Graham, this is all so confusing. Can you give me some time to think? Meet me on the top deck at ten tonight. We can talk; I can't concentrate right now; Peter could be back any minute," she asked, her voice barely above a whisper.

"Ten," Graham echoed, his voice unwavering.

"Wait, you mean the one where Denny?...."

"Yes," replied Sarah.

Graham knew that was strange but didn't want to risk the meeting not happening.

As the door clicked shut behind him, Sarah's breath hitched—ten o'clock— three hours from now. The night would cloak their meeting in darkness and shadows would hide the truth they both harboured. She glanced at the clock, its ticking a metronome to her racing heart. Anticipation coiled in her stomach, tight and insistent. She knew she couldn't be a part of Graham's death, but she knew she was cornered. She had three hours to decide what to do.

Sarah paced her room, her steps soundless. She stopped by the mirror, studying her reflection. Could the others see the guilt etched into her features? Did they notice how her hands shook? She remembered a time before this when usual day-to-day worries would consume her; she wished she could go back and take all those on.

A gust of wind rattled the window, pulling her from her thoughts. The storm was gathering strength, changing back to the norm. She closed her eyes, willing her heartbeat to slow, to match the deceptive calm before nature unleashed its fury.

"Get it together, Sarah," she whispered to her reflection. "You can do this."

She guessed Edward would be alone on the deck, he would not risk anyone else knowing what was going on.

When Peter returned from the gym, the ship seemed quieter, as if holding its breath in anticipation. As he returned to their cabin, a sense of unease gnawed at his insides, an instinctual warning that something was amiss.

Upon entering the room, Peter found Sarah standing by the window, her features etched with a contemplative expression. Her usual warmth was gone.

"Sarah, is everything alright?" Peter's voice cut through the silence, laden with concern and an undercurrent of fear.

"You mean, apart from dealing with having murdered someone?" Sarah said sarcastically.

Peter laughed and shook his head, looking at the ground.

The clock continued its relentless march towards 10 o'clock, each tick a reminder of the impending reckoning awaiting Sarah on the deck. She still didn't know what she was going to do. She had thought of waiting until then, but this was not the kind of thing she should decide on the spot.

Tension coiled in her body like a spring, ready to snap. Her breaths came in shallow gasps as she grappled with the gravity of the situation.

She looked in the mirror and traced the lines etched on her face, markers of a life lived.

Then she made a conscious decision, the most deliberate thing she'd done for days. As she prepared to leave the room to meet Graham and be watched from the shadows by Edward, she took the small, sharp, serrated knife from the breakfast table and put it in her coat pocket.

CHAPTER EIGHTEEN

TUESDAY EVENING

THE EMERALD EMPRESS

DAY FOUR OF THE CRUISE

"Goodnight, love. Do you mind if I get an early night? I'm exhausted," Peter said. He leaned down, brushing his lips against her forehead—a familiar, tender gesture that spoke of years of the similar goodnight.

"Of course not. Goodnight, darling." Sarah forced a smile, her eyes meeting his for a fleeting second. "I might step out for a bit of fresh air later; I don't think I'll sleep," she added, not wanting to make a big deal of it.

"Just be careful, please. Don't go outside," said Peter.

He walked away and disappeared through the door into their bedroom, leaving Sarah sitting silently in the lounge area of their suite.

"Dammit, Graham," she muttered under her breath.

"Why did it have to come to this?"

The choice she had to make was too huge to comprehend.

Sarah sat there in silence, weighing her options. Knowing tonight needed to end with Graham still alive, she owed it to him not to sacrifice him for her safety.

Sarah didn't know how long she'd been sitting there in the dark, but she had decided—she knew what she was going to do—and it was time to leave. With one last glance at the room's stillness, Sarah grabbed her coat and headed for the door.

With each movement, echoing footsteps filled the maze of hallways as she made her way through the corridors. Her eyes darted to a clock hanging on one of the walls, its hands pointing to 9:45 pm. She quickened her pace, knowing she needed to reach the deck before it was too late. As she walked, her mind was consumed with conflicting thoughts and emotions, all centred around Graham. She couldn't deny the deep feelings she had always harboured for him, but what could come of it? A cool breeze blew in from an open window, bringing with it the distant sound of crashing waves and the salty scent of the sea.

As she looked out to sea, a memory surfaced unbidden—a crisp autumn day 25 years ago, with leaves painted in fiery hues drifting down onto the college pathways. She had been waiting, textbooks cradled against her chest, when Graham's familiar figure emerged from the crowd of students.

25 YEARS EARLIER

COLLEGE DAYS

"Mind if I walk you home?" Graham's voice had that lilt of casual elegance even then.

The pair were at college. Sarah knew Graham from school, and she hadn't ever recognised him as the adult he now was.

"Sure," Sarah replied, trying to mask the flutter in her stomach with a smile. They started side by side, her heart beating an erratic dance as the distance closed between them, occasionally bumping into each other.

"Beautiful day, isn't it?" Graham had gestured towards the canopy of red and gold above them. "Though not as beautiful as—"

"Leave it out, Graham." Sarah cut him off, half teasing, half wary. She'd heard the lines before, seen them work their magic on others. It had been a beautiful day, now fading to sunset.

"Can't a guy admire the scenery without an ulterior motive?" he'd shot back with the confidence of someone who had nothing to lose.

They'd walked in easy silence, the rustling of leaves underfoot punctuating their steps.

Then, with a suddenness that caught her off guard, Graham's demeanour shifted. He stopped and turned to face her, his eyes searching hers with an intensity that bordered on desperation.

"Sarah, I—" He hesitated, the playful charm faltering. But she remembered his eyes, the earnestness that coloured his usual confidence.

"Please, don't." She'd felt the words escape her before fully grasping their implication. A pre-emptive strike against whatever confession lay on his tongue.

Graham's mouth had opened, then closed, and something undefinable had passed between them—an acknowledgement of a line drawn, a boundary set.

"Right," he'd said, the word a quiet surrender. With a rueful smile, he'd resumed walking, leaving the unsaid hanging like the autumn fog that would creep in come evening.

But tonight, there was an urgency about him, a hunger that disrupted the rhythm of time.

"Sarah," he began, his voice cutting through the quiet evening once again, "I need to tell you something important."

She glanced over, noting the intense look in his eyes—the one that always forewarned of serious conversation. She braced herself.

"I can't pretend anymore," he confessed, halting under the golden glow of the streetlamp. They stood bathed in its light.

"I really like you, Sarah. I think we could be good for each other deeply, irrevocably."

This was Graham, refined and controlled, laying his soul bare on the pavement where they once talked about college exams and future dreams, rode their bikes, and sold lemonade to passers-by.

Her heart stuttered, a flutter of old affection mingling with the weight of present reality. "Graham," she started, her voice a whisper of conflict, "you know I'm with Peter now."

"Peter?! Bloody Hell, Sarah, he's so dull," Graham scoffed.

Sarah shook her head. "He's safe. I need safe."

He stepped closer, his presence a magnetic force she fought to resist.

"Okay, but that doesn't change how I feel. I'm safe, too. We could be incredible together, Sarah. We could go on adventures, but still be safe and feel like a real team."

But Sarah had built her world alongside another, woven her hopes and plans into the fabric of a life with Peter—a man who offered stability and partnership, who held her when nightmares clawed their way into her sleep.

"Please, Graham." Her tone sharpened with resolve. "Don't do this. It's not right. Peter and I—we're committed to each other."

"Is it commitment, or is it fear?"

His question prodded at her doubts, but she fortified her stance.

"Commitment," she asserted, stepping back from him, from the precipice of a decision that would unravel everything she'd carefully constructed. "And respect—for him, for us."

Graham's expression shifted, the playful glint in his eye dimming. He searched her face, perhaps for a sign of hesitation, a crack in her resolve. But she offered none.

"Then I'll say no more," he relented and nodded, more to himself than to her, and when he finally spoke again, his words were edged with the precision she recognised so well.

"Goodnight, Sarah. I won't mention it again, but I'm yours forever. Wherever we are, whatever we're doing, I'll be with you at the drop of a hat."

"Goodnight, Graham. I'll introduce you to my friend Lucy. I think you'd get on really well." Her reply felt like a verdict as she watched him disappear into the evening, leaving her to grapple with the echo of his confession and the steady beat of a heart torn between what could have been and what must be.

"OK, great, I'll look forward to meeting her. But Sarah, you'll always be my number one," said Graham as he walked away.

Sarah liked him, and she had known for years that she would wonder what had happened if she had made a different decision.

9.50 PM
THE EMERALD EMPRESS
DAY FOUR OF THE CRUISE

Sarah perched on the edge of the plush lounge sofa on the upper deck viewing room, her fingers absentmindedly tracing the embroidered patterns on the cushions. Her mind, a whirlwind of past and present, wouldn't settle. She knew she needed to save Graham from Edward. She had left the room too early and could have done without having to wait. Where was Edward? She knew he would already be watching her and thinking at this point that the plan was going ahead. She played with the knife in her pocket, teasing herself with its blade.

The clock ticked away the seconds, each one a reminder of the tightrope she walked.

She had always loved Graham, in a way. She knew that. She would save him. She had to save him from Edward and accept the consequences.

"Peter can never know," she whispered, her voice barely audible. But the truth was a relentless pursuer, shadowing her every step, waiting for a slip, a crack in her armour.

With a shaky exhale, Sarah stood up, her decision firming with the rise. She needed space to breathe. If she were to navigate the minutes ahead, she'd have to be cunning and decisive. She loved Graham, and it was time to admit it to herself, no matter the cost.

"Be smart, Sarah," she coached herself, "You've survived worse."

Sarah glanced outside to see Graham's silhouette walking across the dark deck.

CHAPTER NINETEEN

TUESDAY NIGHT, 10 PM
THE EMERALD EMPRESS
DAY FOUR OF THE CRUISE

As she emerged into the night air, she took a deep breath and smiled. Graham stood at the railing; his lean silhouette etched against the backdrop of the restless sea. The rain had momentarily stopped.

"Sarah," he greeted, "I wasn't sure you'd come."

"Of course I came," she replied, her words steady.

Graham's eyes held hers, the mischievous glint within them belying the earnest curve of his smile. He had always been able to charm his way through life, from the high-class patrons in his restaurants to the sophisticated guests aboard the cruise ship.

"Let's talk about us," he said, extending a hand towards her.

"Us?" Sarah echoed, allowing herself a small step forward. Her heart felt like it thrummed against her ribs; the anticipation now mingled with something far more dangerous.

Graham's hand found hers, a gesture that might have been tender under different circumstances. But Sarah's attention was pulled away by a flicker of movement in the periphery—a shadow that didn't belong to the deck chairs or the ornate potted plants.

"Sarah," Graham began, his voice laced with an emotion she couldn't afford to reciprocate, "I've been thinking about what our future could be."

"Graham, I need to tell you something,"

She stood at a crossroads. She knew she couldn't let Graham die, and she knew Edward was near. Nervous energy surged through her body, making her hands tremble, and her breath come in quick gasps. This was the defining moment.

"What is it?" he replied, waiting for the words he wanted to hear.

"We're not safe," she said.

"Safe? No one can see us up here."

"No," Sarah uttered, looking around.

She returned her gaze to him, feigning a warmth she did not feel.

"Stay with me," her words were careful, her tone measured, but her mind raced as she saw him for the first time: Edward Smythe, hidden just out of the lamplight.

He stood motionless, his silver hair blending into the darkness, his piercing blue eyes fixed on their exchange.

"I need to tell you something," Sarah whispered.

Sarah's entire body screamed to her to warn Graham of the impending danger, every bone vibrating with urgency. But fear and panic held her captive, her voice trapped in her throat as she watched helplessly; she knew what she needed to do, her hand now on the small knife.

"What is it?" replied Graham, looking hopeful.

Sarah faltered. Her mind was still whirring.

"Do you see us together?" Sarah wanted to buy herself sometime.

Graham nodded eagerly.

"Yes, I see us together beyond this trip. I want you to be part of my world in every possible way. Things are terrible with Lucy."

Sarah needed to keep him talking, maintain this façade for a while longer, and decide what she would do.

"That's quite a confession, Graham." The corners of her mouth lifted slightly. "Do you remember that day you walked me home after college? I think about it all the time."

"You do? I always saw myself with someone like you." His grip tightened around her hand, mistaking her hesitation for shyness.

Despite the balmy night air, Sarah felt a cold sweat form at the base of her neck. Edward's presence felt like an ice shard lodged in her spine. She knew he was ready to strike, but Sarah knew she had the knife.

"Someone like me?" She played along, her heart pounding with a warning.

"Someone who understands the finer things, who appreciates ambition." Graham's eyes searched hers, hungry for validation.

"Perhaps," Sarah whispered, allowing herself to lean closer. Her skin prickled with defiance and desperation.

"Maybe," Sarah murmured, her breath a whisper against the sea breeze. She stepped forward into Graham's embrace, her arms wrapping around him with tenderness. His smell filled her senses. A mix of citrus and cedar.

"Sarah," Graham sighed, his voice a low thrum of contentment as he held her close.

"It's going to be ok," Her words were velvet caresses, lulling him into a sense of security.

Her nimble and determined fingers found their way into the pocket of his tailored jacket. The smooth surface of his phone grazed her fingertips, and with a subtle pinch, she freed it from its confines.

"Us, together, it's..." Graham began, his thoughts trailing off as Sarah pulled back slightly, looking up at him with an expression artfully crafted to convey interest and affection.

"Special," she finished for him, her gaze locked onto his, ensuring his attention never wavered from her face, "It's always been special, Graham."

"Yes," he replied, a hint of relief as he mistook her engagement for agreement.

In one fluid motion, as though adjusting her stance, Sarah shifted, allowing Graham's phone to slip from her hand into her coat pocket. It was a masterful act, unnoticed by Graham, who remained trapped by the ruse of intimacy.

"Sarah, you're...you're incredible," Graham whispered.

"Am I?" she asked, her voice a soft murmur carrying a weight he couldn't comprehend. She now held Graham's phone in one hand, and the knife in the other.

"Yes," he affirmed, "You truly are."

"Let's walk a bit," Sarah suggested, her arm linking with his.

She felt like the darkness had now taken over her.

Dread clawed at her insides, yet she walked on; she knew she was still prepared for every outcome. She knew she should tell Graham about the impending danger and accept the consequences for what she'd done to Denny, but she couldn't.

She needed to save herself.

They strolled, Sarah's fingers lightly gripping Graham's arm.

"Look at the stars tonight," she remarked, tilting her head upwards, though her eyes were not on the sky but scanning the shadows, thinking about their ideal placement.

They were now on the edge of the deck, next to the railing where she had pushed Denny.

"Beautiful," Graham agreed, but his gaze stayed fixed on her, captivated by a future he thought was within his grasp.

Sarah caught another movement in her peripheral vision. Edward stood there, as still as the night, a statue carved of cold expectation.

Sarah couldn't look him in the eye and couldn't witness the last moments of Graham's life.

She already knew that she would replay these moments in her mind forever. She edged Graham closer to where Edward lurked.

"Fresh air does wonders," she continued, feigning a relaxed tone while her pulse thrummed in her ears.

"Doesn't it just?" Graham said, leaning over the railing to breathe deeply.

It was time. Sarah extricated herself from Graham's hold with a practised smile and stepped back without looking at him.

"All yours," she whispered through lips that barely moved, her message for Edward alone.

Graham turned toward her, a confused question lingering in his expression. He then looked at Edward and back at Sarah, confusion on his face. But before a word could tumble from his lips, Sarah pivoted on her heel, placed the phone on the nearby bench, and didn't look back.

She had barely taken two steps when the scream shattered the night—a visceral, primal sound that ripped through the night. Only three people would have heard it, Edward, Sarah, and Graham, knowing something had been happening all along.

Graham's final cry for help broke through the night. It was followed by a heavy splash, the dark waters below claiming what was offered without remorse.

The chill that then gripped Sarah was not from the ocean breeze; it was born of something darker that crept into her soul and wrapped its icy fingers around her. She stopped in her tracks, her breath catching in her throat, the echoes of Graham's terror reverberating in the hollow space left behind. She looked back and saw Edward's imposing figure, where Graham had stood. She knew what had taken place, and it could never be undone. Sarah then felt a fear for herself, what was stopping Edward from now killing her?

Sarah stumbled down the steps, her legs threatening to give way beneath her. Hot and relentless tears spilt over her cheeks, blurring the world into a dizzying array of lights and shadows.

"God, what have I done?" she choked out, her words soaked in guilt and swallowed by the night. She hadn't decided to go through with it until the last minute. She took the knife from her pocket and looked at the path she hadn't taken. She screamed and threw it back up the stairs towards the ocean.

Although she hadn't seen it, the image of Graham's face, contorted in terror before being swallowed by the dark waters, seared into her memory. She knew his face so well, so she could imagine it. She thought about how scared Graham must have been. He would have had seconds to consider what Sarah had done, seconds to know he was going to die.

"Sarah, focus," she whispered, struggling to corral her spiralling thoughts. Each decision was laced with the never-ending processing she would have to go through. Now, she bore secrets that could shatter lives, including her own. The warm-hearted woman who had once sought to heal was complicit in a plot ending in genuine harm.

Sarah plunged into the shadows, the inky blackness of the lower deck swallowing her whole. She leaned against the cool metal wall, its surface a balm to her flushed cheeks.

"Keep it together," she whispered, each word punctuated by the quiet sob she fought to suppress. Her fingers trembled as they brushed across her face, erasing the traces of vulnerability that had no place in what was to come.

The woman who thrived in the light and mended the broken spirits of others now clung to darkness as an ally.

CHAPTER TWENTY

TUESDAY NIGHT

THE EMERALD EMPRESS

DAY FOUR OF THE CRUISE

The ship's deck was dark, with the only light coming from the pale moon above. The storm had so far masked the moon for most of the voyage. Sarah clutched her shawl around her shoulders as she approached the door to their cabin.

She entered the room quietly, careful not to disturb Peter, who had fallen asleep earlier in the evening. As she closed the door behind her, her gaze fell upon her husband's peaceful form, and a pang of guilt tightened her chest. She envied how Peter slept. What she had done tonight was for him; the only route she could take would end in them being together.

Sarah's hands trembled as she lowered herself onto the edge of the bed. She clasped them tightly in her lap, trying to still their shaking. Deep breaths, she reminded herself. In and out. Slow and steady.

"Sarah?" Peter's voice was thick with sleep. "Everything alright?"

She swallowed hard, forcing a calm she didn't feel into her voice. "Yes, just... restless. My walk didn't tire me out as much as I thought it would. Go back to sleep, darling."

Peter mumbled something unintelligible and rolled over.

How long could she keep this facade up? How long before the truth came crashing down around her? She knew she just needed to get off this ship. Sarah closed her eyes. One breath at a time, she told herself. Just make it through one moment at a time.

2 AM, WEDNESDAY MORNING
THE EMERALD EMPRESS
DAY FIVE OF THE CRUISE

A sudden, frantic pounding on the door shattered the fragile calm. Sarah jolted upright; she hadn't entirely drifted off but was in a dream state. She stumbled over to the door, dragging on her dressing gown.

As she flung it open, Lucy stumbled in, her face a mask of anguish. Tears streaked her cheeks, leaving glistening trails in the dim light.

"Sarah," Lucy choked out, her voice raw with emotion. "It's Graham. He... he..."

Sarah instinctively wrapped her arms around her friend, drawing her close. "Shh, it's okay. What's happened? An argument?" Sarah pretended that she didn't know what had really happened.

Lucy pulled back, fumbling with her phone. Her trembling fingers struggled to unlock the screen. "He sent me this," she whispered, thrusting the device at Sarah.

Sarah's eyes widened as she read the message. The words blurred before her, but their meaning was unmistakable.

TEXT MESSAGE:
I killed Denny, I broke, we argued, I pushed him over.
I can't live with what I've done.
I'm sorry, Lucy. Goodbye, I love you.

Sarah's mind reeled. This couldn't be happening. She knew the truth, but how could she explain without implicating herself? She had killed Denny, not Graham.

“Oh, Lucy,” she breathed, struggling to steady her voice. “I... I don't know what to say.”

Lucy collapsed against Sarah, her body wracked with sobs, silently contorting as she cried. “What do we do, Sarah? What if he really...? He’s not in our room.”

Sarah stroked her friend's hair, buying time as she frantically tried to formulate a response. The walls of deceit were closing in, threatening to suffocate her.

Sarah took a deep breath, steeling herself. “We need to alert security,” she said, surprisingly calm despite the turmoil. “They have to find Graham before... before anything happens. I’m sure this is a cry for help; he wouldn’t do anything silly.”

Lucy nodded frantically, wiping her tears with the back of her hand. "Yes, yes, of course. I'll call them right away."

As Lucy frantically tapped on her phone, Sarah's mind spun with thoughts. She knew the truth–Graham was innocent of Denny's death. However, revealing that knowledge would only lead to more questions, which she couldn't answer without exposing her involvement. Sarah knew Edward had sent the text from Graham's phone; he must have known or guessed the passcode. That was the only way to ensure that Sarah would never be suspected of Denny's murder.

Within minutes, the ship's security team swarmed the corridor once more outside their cabin. Sarah watched from the doorway as people in crisp uniforms rushed past, their voices low due to the late hour.

"They'll find him, won't they?" Lucy asked, her voice small and frightened.

Sarah nodded, not trusting herself to speak. She felt torn, relief and guilt warring within her. With Graham taking complete responsibility for Denny, her secret was now only with one person, Edward.

"I should've seen this coming," Lucy murmured, breaking the tense silence. "Graham's been so... distant lately. So, unlike himself, and I knew Denny would wind him up."

Sarah knew precisely why Graham had been acting strangely. Graham had feelings for Sarah; he had for a long time, and maybe he would use this cruise to tell her that, but she couldn't reveal the truth. Instead, she forced a comforting smile. "You couldn't have known, Lucy. None of us could have predicted this."

The lie tasted bitter, but Sarah swallowed it down. She had come too far to falter now. As the chaos unfolded around her, Sarah made her choice. She would keep her silence, protect herself, and hope that, somehow, this nightmare would end.

As Sarah continued her restless pacing, Peter entered the room, his face etched with concern. His eyes darted between Sarah and Lucy, a question forming on his lips.

"Sarah," he said, his voice low and tense, "can I speak with you for a moment?"

Sarah nodded. She followed Peter to the far corner of the room, away from Lucy's earshot.

"Did you have anything to do with this?" Peter asked, his eyes searching hers.

Sarah stared silently back at Peter.

Peter's gaze hardened. "I know you killed Denny, Sarah. This means that the message from Graham isn't truc. Why would hc have sent that before he jumped? Was he covering up for you? Did you tell him?"

Sarah's breath caught in her throat. She shook her head, forcing her voice to remain steady.

"No, of course not. I've only told you. Why would you even ask that? I don't know why Graham would send that message; maybe it was one last act of mischief. However, it's happened. I'll get away with it if we keep quiet."

The world seemed to tilt beneath Sarah's feet. She gripped the wall for support, her mind reeling. She knew she wanted Peter to know, but couldn't find the words. She would tell him one day, but she wanted to protect him right now.

Sarah glanced over at Lucy, who was still huddled on the bed, lost in her thoughts. She turned back to Peter, her voice barely above a whisper.

"I'll explain everything, I promise. But not here, not now."

Peter nodded, his jaw set. "I'm going to join the search. We'll talk about this later."

Sarah turned to Lucy, forcing a comforting smile. "It's going to be alright," she said, her voice steadier than she felt.
"Everyone is looking for him."
Lucy nodded absently; her eyes distant. The door opened slowly, attracting their attention. Terri entered the room, her face etched with concern.
"Any news?" Terri asked, settling beside them.
Sarah shook her head, guilt gnawing at her insides. "Nothing yet," she managed.
Terri looked at both of them with the expression that she wanted to say something.
"I hate to say it, but...you know I'm glad Denny's gone, so I'm grateful to Graham if that's what he did," she said, her voice barely above a whisper.
Lucy's head snapped up; her eyes suddenly sharp. "Graham isn't gone, and he didn't kill Denny," she insisted. "He'll be found alive. You'll see."
"Terri, this isn't the time or place." Sarah looked at Terri like a mother telling off a child. Terri nodded and looked at the floor.
"Lucy," Sarah began cautiously, "it's okay to be upset. We're here for you."
Lucy's face relaxed slightly. "I'm fine," she said, her tone clipped. "Graham is fine. End of discussion."

Sarah exchanged a glance with Terri, both unsettled by Lucy's demeanour.

The heavy wooden door swung open, creaking on its hinges and startling everyone. Peter stepped inside, his footsteps heavy and weary. His usually cheerful face was now drawn and gaunt, with dark circles under his eyes. Sarah's hands trembled as she searched his expression for any sign of news and how she needed to react to it. The air in the room seemed to thicken as they waited for Peter to speak.

"Anything?" she asked, her voice barely above a whisper.

The storm raged outside like a thousand cannons, shaking the ground beneath Peter's feet. He glanced out the window, thinking it was picking up again despite having cooled down for the last few hours. A blinding flash of lightning momentarily illuminated his face, revealing his expression contorted with fear and desperation.

Peter shook his head, running a hand through his messy hair. "Nothing. There's no sign of him."

The room seemed to darken by the second.

Lucy let out a strangled sob, burying her face in her hands. Sarah moved to comfort her, but Lucy shrugged off her touch.

"I need some air," Lucy muttered, rushing out of the room.

As the door clicked shut behind her, Terri cleared her throat. "I should go check on Lucy," she said, excusing herself from the suffocating atmosphere.

Alone with Peter, Sarah sank onto the bed, exhaustion seeping into her bones. She knew that now was the time.

She took a deep breath, steeling herself.

"Peter, there's something I need to tell you," Sarah said, her voice wavering slightly. "It's about Graham's murder."

Peter looked up in complete shock. "Oh Fuck, Sarah, not him too."

"No!" she replied. "What do you think I am?"

"So what? What do you know about it? You said murder, so he didn't kill himself?" Peter replied, completely broken, with an angry tinge to his voice.

Sarah sat down across from him, wringing her hands. "I... I helped Edward Smythe. He revealed to me that he knew I'd killed Denny. He has the footage."

"Oh god," Peter put his head in his hands.

"He said that if I helped him to kill Graham, he'd get rid of the footage. I got Graham's phone for him, so I presume he could send the message..."

“You what?” Peter's eyes widened in shock.

“Why the hell would Edward want to kill Graham? They were friends?”

“Edward wanted revenge. Graham had sunk his parents' business years ago and ruined them. Edward’s dad killed himself. Edward was determined to make him pay.”

Peter leaned back, processing this revelation. Sarah waited for his reaction. Would he condemn her? Turn her in?

“Why didn’t Graham mention this? He never even said he’d met Edward’s parents. He never mentioned that at all.” Peter seemed confused.

After a long moment, Peter reached out and took Sarah’s hand. “I understand why you did it. You’ve saved yourself, saved us. We're in the clear as long as people believe the story. Are you sure Edward will stick to his word and destroy the evidence?”

“I had no choice, Peter; I had to take him for his word. I just need to make sure he destroys that hard drive.”

“Poor Lucy,” Peter whispered. “But we’re in this together, okay? We roll with the punches.”

Relief washed over Sarah. She squeezed Peter's hand, grateful for his undying support.

"We'll figure this out," Peter assured her, though uncertainty shadowed his eyes. "Edward has just as much to lose as we do if the truth gets out. I'm sure he'll keep quiet. Oh, poor Lucy."

Sarah nodded, knowing her best friend was now a widow and that she had contributed to that. She knew their marriage wasn't perfect, but she knew Lucy would be devastated. Sarah then had a sinking feeling that this secret would come back to haunt them. One way or another, there would be a price to pay.

"I'm going to try to get some rest," Peter said, his voice flat. "You should, too; it's the middle of the night. I've got you. "

Sarah watched as he disappeared into the bathroom. When the door closed, she reached for her phone with trembling hands. Her fingers hovered over Edward Smythe's contact information. Should she risk it? The evidence of her involvement still existed, a constant threat hanging over her head. She had upheld her part of the bargain and wanted to ensure Edward kept to his.

She scrolled through her messages, her heart racing. One wrong move could unravel everything.

But the uncertainty was eating her alive. She needed answers, reassurance that her part in this nightmare would remain hidden.

Sarah's thumb hesitated over the message button. Was contacting Edward worth the risk? Or would it only entangle her further in his web of deceit? She didn't want any records of them contacting each other, records that would later become important, but she also knew that it could be explained away with the loss of their friend.

The soft glow of her phone screen illuminated her conflicted features as she stared at the screen.

"No," she whispered to herself, shaking her head. "I can't."

With a decisive swipe, she closed the messaging app and set the phone face-down on the nightstand.

She glanced out of the port hole across the room, a black circle without sunlight.

She turned onto her side, curling into herself as if to shield her body from the crushing guilt. The room's darkness seemed to close around her, pulsing and taunting her.

"Get it together, Sarah, we're almost free," she muttered, willing herself to find some calm.

But peace eluded her, replaced by a constant stream of what-ifs and worst-case scenarios.

As she lay there, Sarah wondered if she had already sealed her fate when she pushed Denny overboard. The memory of that impulsive act haunted her, a constant reminder of the darkness she harboured beneath her nurturing exterior. Even after everything Denny had done to the women around him, she was fully aware that she was in the wrong, too.

Sleep, it seemed, would be a luxury she couldn't afford tonight.

CHAPTER TWENTY-ONE

FIVE YEARS EARLIER
THE RITZ HOTEL, LONDON

The lavish Palm Court of the Ritz Hotel in London sparkled with cascading ornate chandeliers and the glittering attire of its bustling guests. It was the launch of Graham Winslow's restaurant menus for the luxurious Emerald Empress cruise ship.

The Palm Court, dressed in vibrant floral arrangements and signature green palms, was a sight to behold. Intricate golden designs adorned the ceiling, catching the light and casting a warm glow over the room. The beautifully carved mirrors lining the walls acted as windows, creating the illusion that the space was even larger and more enchanting than it already was. In the background, a string quartet played soft melodies, their instruments hidden from view but their music filling every corner of the room. This room was the definition of elegance.

Feeling beautiful but self-conscious in her designer black gown, Lucy Winslow navigated the crowd of familiar faces, her pearl necklace resting delicately against her collarbone. Tonight, she was playing the hostess for her husband, a role she had never wanted or was comfortable with. She reached for a glass of champagne from a passing waiter when her eyes met those of a man across the room who appeared to be glancing in her direction. Their gazes locked, and time slowed as they took each other in. The man then slowly started to walk over.

"Ah, Lucy," said Edward Smythe, approaching her confidently. His suit looked expensive under the chandelier lights. "You look stunning tonight. Graham has told me so much about you."

"Thank you, Mr. Smythe," she replied, feeling a flutter in her chest at the intensity of his blue eyes. "It's a pleasure to meet you."

"Likewise. Please, call me Edward." He lifted a glass of champagne to his lips, his gaze never leaving hers.

The delicate scent of lemon and bergamot wafted from the elegant tea service, mingling with the soft murmur of conversation. The party served hot drinks and champagne, which Lucy imagined would eventually transition into just champagne.

"Lucy, it really is a pleasure to meet you." He took her hand, his lips brushing against her knuckles in a gentlemanly gesture.

She returned the smile, her eyes sparkling with a hint of mischief. "The pleasure is all mine, Edward."

As they took their seats, Lucy couldn't help but notice how Edward's suit hugged his trim frame. He had aged well. She had seen him a few times since Graham had been involved with him, but never this close-up.

"Graham is a lucky man."

Lucy laughed, a musical sound that turned heads. "Oh, Edward, you flatter me. But let's not talk about Graham. I'm much more interested in hearing about you."

She leaned forward, her fingers toying with the string of pearls at her throat. It was a calculated move she had perfected over years of navigating high society. Men like Edward were all the same - easily manipulated, with a coy smile and a hint of cleavage.

Edward's eyes followed the movement of her fingers. "There's not much to tell, I'm afraid. My work keeps me busy, as always."

"But surely a man of your stature must have time for a little fun now and then?" Lucy arched an eyebrow, her lips curving into a playful smirk.

He chuckled, shaking his head.

"My business ventures are fun."

Lucy couldn't shake the feeling that Edward was holding something back as their next drink arrived on a silver tray. There was a tension in his shoulders, a guardedness in his expression. She would have to tread carefully.

But for now, she would play the game - laughing at his jokes and hanging on his every word. Flirting with Edward was a familiar dance she knew by heart.

Their conversation flowed seamlessly from one topic to another, punctuated by moments of charged silence. Lucy was captivated by Edward's enigmatic charm, her pulse quickening with each word he spoke.

"I don't think I've ever met someone that owns a cruise ship, Edward. You're obviously doing very well for yourself."

"Well, thank you, but your husband's done quite well for himself, hasn't he?

I'm honoured he has agreed to design the menus for my cruise ship, The Emerald Empress, the lady in my life." Edward said, glancing around the opulent ballroom.

"Ah yes, The Emerald Empress, I've heard about it." Lucy hadn't heard about it.

"Yes, it's smaller than I'd like, but it'll do." Edward smiled.

"What about the boat?" Lucy knew she had probably gone too far.

Edward smiled and gave her a wink.

"We're going to get on just fine," replied Edward, showing he was comfortable with this banter.

"But anyway, Graham has done well for himself."

"Uh, yes, he has," she responded, her smile faltering slightly. She thought, "I wish it were enough," but didn't dare say it aloud.

"Well, I'd better get back to my duties; I'm sure I'll see you later?" Edward said.

"Of course," Lucy said in the most disappointed tone.

As Lucy took another sip, the warmth of the alcohol spread through her body, bringing with it a sense of detachment from the lively festivities and chattering conversations around her.

She felt like an outsider, observing from afar rather than fully participating in the merriment. The clinking of glasses and laughter seemed distant and hazy as she sank deeper into her thoughts and emotions.

Earlier in the evening, she had tried to converse with others, but now found herself standing alone in a secluded corner of the room.

Edward again gracefully pivoted and glided across the room, his movements fluid like water. He landed smoothly next to Lucy, his presence as captivating as a flame in the darkness.

"Tell me," Edward said, his voice lowering conspiratorially, "Is there anything you desire, Lucy? Something your heart yearns for, perhaps?"

"Edward..." The vulnerability in her voice surprised even her, even more than Edward's direct question. She hesitated, glancing away, then looked back into his piercing eyes. "I... I'm not sure."

"Sometimes, the heart knows what it wants, even when the mind is uncertain." He paused, searching her face for a reaction. "You'll know when the time comes."

Lucy felt herself drowning in his gaze, her heart pounding.

She couldn't quite put her finger on it, but something about Edward Smythe intrigued and terrified her.

"Excuse me," she said abruptly, putting down her empty champagne flute. "I should return to my husband."

"Of course," he replied, a hint of defeat in his voice. But as she turned to leave, he added, "Until we meet again, Lucy."

"Graham," Lucy interrupted his conversation with a group of well-dressed strangers.

"Darling! You'll never guess who's here," said Graham, "Come with me, excuse me, please," Graham grabbed Lucy by the hand and dragged her away from the group he'd been talking to.

She followed behind him, still holding his hand.

"Here she is! Can you believe it?" Graham stepped aside.

"Oh my god! Alice!" Lucy hadn't seen Alice since they said goodbye in the park when she and Denny were about to travel to New York.

They hadn't had too much contact with Denny, but they knew the pair had been divorced.

"Well, I'd better keep circulating; I'll leave you both to catch up." Graham wandered back into the bustling crowd.

Lucy and Alice found two chairs on the edge of the room and made small talk, a brief summary of the time they hadn't seen each other.

"I must say," said Alice, "I am surprised to see you and Graham still together."

"Why would you say that?" Lucy was defensive.

"You always seemed like too much of a free spirit for someone like Graham," Alice said, wondering if she had stepped over the mark.

"Well, sometimes we adapt to the hand we're dealt." Lucy conceded.

"That's what I thought with Denny. I was sure that New York would cure us, but it was a distraction for a few months; once the novelty wore off, he returned to his old ways." Alice looked down.

"Oh, Alice," said Lucy, "we were all worried about that. Are you okay?"

"Yeah, I'm fine. I'm moving on, and I've never felt this free." Alice smiled genuinely. "I just wish I'd done it sooner."

"I know Alice, I just can't leave him," the alcohol was helping the words slip from Lucy's lips.

"I always thought that with Denny, but I wish I could turn back the clock; as every day ticked by, I knew it wasn't right, but I didn't do anything, and I regret it now," Alice confessed.

"You know Alice, some days I just wish something would just happen to him so I could move on."

Alice looked shocked at this statement.

"I think you've had too much to drink, but I want you to think about it," said Alice.

"I will, I promise," replied Lucy.

"Every day you're with him is a day wasted. You need to be free, darling." Alice hugged Lucy and stood to walk away.

"Do you see Sarah much?" Alice enquired.

"No, not too much," Lucy's face dropped.

"I'm meeting her next weekend; she was always so good at listening. I'm going to pour my heart out to her, tell her everything about what happened with Denny," said Alice.

"She is good at listening," Lucy smiled.

"Well, I'd better go and find the guy I'm here with," Alice said, looking around the room. "I'm sure I'll see you again; Edward has promised me a ride on his cruise ship."

"Lovely to see you, Alice," Lucy said, disappointed that Edward hadn't yet invited her on the cruise ship.

Alice disappeared into the crowd, and Lucy sat there, thinking about her advice.

Lucy fidgeted with her fifth or sixth empty champagne flute. She glanced at Edward, his enigmatic presence drawing her attention away from Graham's speech, which drifted on in the background. Lucy, this time, moved towards Edward, sideways through the listening crowd, her movements becoming more confident with alcohol.

“Edward,” she whispered, leaning closer, “I feel so... trapped.”

“Trapped?” he asked, his voice a mixture of concern and curiosity.

“By my life with Graham,” she admitted, her words barely audible as the crowd applauded her husband's speech.

“He controls every aspect of my life. I don't even know who I am anymore.”

“Ah, Lucy,” Edward said softly, his eyes filled with empathy, “it's terrible to lose oneself in another's shadow.”

“Sometimes, I dream of a different life,” she confessed, her gaze darting back to her husband for a moment before returning to Edward. “A life where I can breathe and make my own choices.”

Edward hesitated, then gently brushed his fingers against her hand.

"Perhaps we could find a way to stay connected despite your husband's watchful eye. A secret correspondence, if you will. I think we could be mutually beneficial to each other."

"Really?" Lucy asked, her eyes widening with surprise and excitement.

"But what if Graham finds out?"

"Leave that to me, ok?" he assured her, his soothing and dangerous smile.

"Ok," she repeated, her voice trembling with the weight of her decision.

"I suppose you're right."

"Good," Edward replied, giving her hand a reassuring squeeze.

"Then it's settled. We'll keep in touch. And who knows what possibilities may arise?"

Lucy felt a shiver run down her spine. Was this indeed the path she wanted to take? But as she glanced at Graham, surrounded by his adoring friends and colleagues and utterly oblivious to her inner turmoil, she knew she needed something more.

"Alright," she agreed, her voice barely audible. "Let's keep in touch."

"Excellent," Edward whispered, his eyes shining with intrigue.

"Our little secret, Lucy. Just between us."

As the applause died down and the guests began to mingle, Lucy felt a strange mixture of fear and exhilaration coursing through her veins. She had taken the first step into the unknown, and there was no turning back now.

As the night wore on, Lucy clutched another glass of champagne, the bubbles having long gone flat, instinctively knowing she needed to slow her drinking, but she wasn't strong enough to stop altogether. Her vision clouded as she leaned against a pillar, swaying slightly. Her elegant stance was gone; this was now more about staying upright.

The vast gravity of the evening stretched out before her, with only a handful of fleeting conversations to break up the solitude, except for Edward. This night was all about her meeting him. She longed for a meaningful connection, a deep conversation that would fill the void inside her.

Edward again appeared at her side, steadying her with a firm hand on her elbow.

"Careful now," he said, his voice low and smooth. "We wouldn't want you to take a tumble." His grip on her was way too tight.

"Thank you," she murmured, attempting to collect herself.

"Tell me something," Lucy slurred, her inhibitions lowered by the alcohol coursing through her veins. "Your cruise ship,"

"Yes, I told you earlier, the love of my life," Edward replied, his eyes glinting in the dim light. "The Emerald Empress is my pride and joy."

"Have you ever…" She hesitated, as if struggling to find the right words.

"Have you ever had someone disappear on one of your ships?"

"What do you mean?" Edward looked surprised.

"You know," said Lucy,

"Has anyone been on a cruise and just fallen off the ship?"

Edward's expression remained unchanged, his eyes never leaving hers. "It has been known to happen," he admitted, his tone casual.

"People can be quite careless, you see. They drink too much and lean over the railing for fresh air…only to plunge into the icy depths below. The North Sea is not somewhere you want to be in the water."

"Isn't that…awful?" Lucy asked, her voice trembling as she tried to comprehend the enormity of his statement.

"Life is full of tragedies, my dear; the winners don't even need to swim," he responded, his voice devoid of emotion.

She felt a chill run down her spine again, unsure whether it was from the alcohol or the unsettling conversation.

"I feel so trapped, and I think sometimes my life would be better without Graham, but I just can't leave him," Lucy said, ashamed at her admission.

"Well, let's keep talking. I think you could help me, too," Edward said with a smirk.

She stared at him, searching for reassurance, but instead, she saw only an enigmatic glint in his eyes.

The soft melody of the string quartet floated through the air as Lucy stared into Edward's penetrating blue eyes. The line between curiosity and apprehension seemed to blur, his presence alluring and unnervingly intense.

"Edward," she began hesitantly, her voice a mere whisper above the din of the party.

"Why are you so interested in me?"

"Lucy," he replied with a cryptic smile. Leaning closer to her ear, his warm breath brushing against her skin, he said,

"It's not every day I meet someone who captures my attention quite like you."

“Is that so?” she asked, excited at his proximity. She tried to ignore the lingering unease from their prior conversation, focusing instead on the thrill of their secret connection.

“Indeed,” he said, straightening up and meeting her gaze again.

“There's something about you, Lucy Winslow, that I find utterly captivating.”

She blushed at his words, but couldn't help the slight grin that formed on her lips. “And what if your fascination puts me in danger? What if Graham were to suspect something?”

“Ah, well,” Edward mused, the corners of his mouth lifting ever so slightly. “Sometimes, one must take risks to achieve true happiness, wouldn't you agree? Maybe Graham could fall off my ship, and we could make new lives,” he laughed, obviously not seriously.

“Perhaps…” she murmured, her eyes darting away from his momentarily as she considered his statement.

“But is this risk worth it? Will you be there to protect me if things go wrong?” she laughed.

Edward still thought Lucy was drunk and joking, so they played with her bad taste.

"Of course, my dear," he answered smoothly, his tone reassuring. "You have my word."

"Your word," she echoed, knowing that although this man was enigmatic, he couldn't be trusted.

"Lucy," Edward said, gently grasping her hand. "I understand your apprehension, but trust that my intentions towards you are honourable."

"Is that a promise?" she asked with a teasing lilt, trying to dispel the lingering shadows of doubt.

"Indeed it is," he replied, his eyes locked on hers. "I vow to be by your side, no matter what obstacles we face."

"Very well," she whispered, allowing herself to be drawn into the vortex of his magnetic gaze. As the room swirled around them in a blur of glitz and glamour, Lucy Winslow found herself willingly entangled in the enigma that was Edward Smythe.

Edward led Lucy away from the raucous party, their hands urgently entwined. As they reached a secluded corner of the venue, Lucy felt her heart race in anticipation.

"Where does this lead us, Edward?" she asked anxiously, her voice barely audible above the din.

"Only time will tell," he replied.

"Then let's toast to our secret alliance," she declared, raising her glass to his in a daring and desperate gesture. She knew she had drunk way too much now.

As their glasses met with a soft chime, Lucy felt a thrill fuelled by the intoxicating combination of fear and excitement coursing through her veins. Edward could much more easily take his drink, keeping one eye on Lucy and one eye on Graham's location. Lucy knew that her life would never be the same again from that moment on.

"Here's to the unknown," whispered Edward, his eyes alight with a fire she couldn't quite decipher.

"Indeed," she agreed, taking a deep breath as they downed their drinks in unison.

"So, let's meet up, let's have a serious chat. Here's my number." Edward handed over his sleek business card, printed in gold leaf on one side but with a handwritten number on the other.

"I'll call," said Lucy.

As they stood there, lost in the moment's intensity, neither could have predicted the far-reaching consequences of their clandestine union. For now, all that mattered was the irresistible pull between them, a bond forged in secrecy and shrouded in mystery.

With a final lingering glance, Edward vanished into the crowd, leaving Lucy to ponder the significance of their fateful encounter.

"Keep in touch." Edward mouthed the words to Lucy.

As Lucy re-entered the party, she felt a sense of apprehension mingled with an undeniable curiosity.

The thought lingered in Lucy's mind, a heavy weight that she tried to push away. She knew that her inevitable fate was to contact Edward; it was just a matter of when. She could almost hear his voice calling out to her, urging her to surrender to their forbidden connection. With a sigh, she closed her eyes and let the thought consume her, embracing the bittersweet longing for what could never be. Tomorrow would come soon enough, and she would have to face the reality of their situation. But for now, in this moment of stillness and solitude, she allowed herself to indulge in the fantasy of him once more.

CHAPTER TWENTY-TWO

WEDNESDAY MORNING
THE EMERALD EMPRESS
DAY FIVE OF THE CRUISE

Sarah jolted awake. She wasn't sure how long she'd been asleep, but it wasn't long. The text message was a lie.

With no time to waste, she hurled herself out of bed, her fingers fumbling with the buttons of her blouse. Each second throbbed with urgency, and her mind replayed the twisted narrative she had sold to them all.

The image of Graham's lifeless body haunted her thoughts as they had all night. She couldn't escape the questions that swirled around her. Where was he now? Was he floating? Or had he sunk to the ocean bed? His unknown fate played in her mind. The man she had known since college was dead. But in the deep parts of her mind, Sarah knew she was proud of herself, proud that she had saved herself. She had never been someone to put herself first.

Slipping into her shoes, Sarah did not glance at the mirror; her reflection would only show a woman on the edge and how part of her despised who she would now be forever.

Sarah needed to see Edward.

She needed the closure.

In the still morning, the corridor to Edward's quarters felt endless and oppressively narrow. As she approached, her steps quickened, and her breathing shallowed. The quiet, slow hum of the ship seemed to mock her racing pulse.

She arrived, her hand raised in a fist before realising it, and knocked sharply.

As the door swung open, a vision of elegance and control appeared. It was Edward, his stance rigid, like that of a soldier at attention. His piercing gaze locked onto Sarah's, but she held her own without flinching.

"Edward, I want to see it destroyed," she declared, her voice steady despite the tremor threatening to betray her nerves.

"Of course, Sarah," he replied, his voice smooth like polished stone.

"Please, come in."

Sarah noticed that he had said this louder than necessary and called her name as if to announce her arrival to someone else.

He stepped aside, and she entered.

Sarah swept across Edward's study, locking her eyes onto a large screen that splintered the room's shadows with a quilt of live surveillance feeds. Each square on the screen pulsed with the secrets of the Emerald Empress, a digital heartbeat monitoring the vessel's veins.

"Everything," Edward began, his tone even as he gestured to the screen, "is stored on one hard drive. Destroying it will erase the footage. Permanently. You may think, 'Why doesn't he make a copy?' but I don't want these files out there any more than you do, Sarah; they don't reflect well on me either."

Edward held up the drive, the only object in the world that connected Sarah to this mess. It was so small—not much bigger than a hardback book—but had huge implications.

"Then let's not waste any more time," Sarah urged, feeling the weight of each second passing.

Edward paused, his eyes narrowing slightly. "I'm beginning to think that might not be in my best interest," he mused.

Turning back to the screen, with his back to Sarah, he placed the hard drive back in its holder next to the control unit.

"You see, I don't think I could ever go into something like this alone."

Before Sarah could challenge his hesitation, some movement took her attention in her peripheral vision, and a door slowly creaked open as if blown by the wind.

"Ah, here you are!" Edward smirked.

"Just in time, Sarah, say hello to the mastermind of this whole thing."

First, a hand reached around the edge of the door, and she stepped out, relishing every moment of her entrance.

Lucy's devilish smile, sharp as a knife, cut through the lingering tension in the room.

"Hello, sweetheart. Are you surprised to see me? Oh, and Edward, you won't be destroying anything," she chimed in with a tone dripping with satisfaction. The air seemed to crackle around her as she confidently took control of the situation. She walked towards them with a confident slink Sarah had never seen before.

"Lucy? Why are you here so early? And in a dressing gown?" Sarah asked, but knew the answer.

"Surprised to see me, darling? You didn't expect me to sleep alone with my husband floating in the ocean? What if I got scared in the night?" Lucy tilted her head, her blonde locks shimmering against the dim light.

"I also heard every word. I think it's rather naïve to believe I would let you make all this... disappear."

Sarah's eyes widened in shock as she took in Lucy's expression. She knew this situation was now far from over. It was a look in Lucy she had never seen before, one that really scared her. There was an unhinged wildness to it, a sense of madness and unbridled fury simmering just beneath the surface. Sarah couldn't help but feel a pang of fear as she looked into her friend's eyes, wondering what could have caused such a drastic change in her demeanour.

Lucy's face remained crazed as she stared at Sarah, her voice low and steady. "You don't understand, do you? I had to do it. I had to get rid of Graham."

Sarah shook her head in disbelief.

"But why, Lucy? Why would you want your own husband dead?"

Lucy let out a bitter laugh.

"You have no idea what it was like being married to that man: constant control and suffocating expectations. I felt like I was drowning, day after day, year after year. Then I met the man of my dreams, and we hatched this plan together, the only way we could be together." She turned to smile at Edward, who smiled back. She began pacing the room, her movements sharp and agitated.

"Graham thought he owned me and could mould me into his perfect little wife. But I had dreams, Sarah. Dreams that he would never let me pursue." Lucy's voice rose, the words tumbling out in a fierce confession.

Sarah reached out, trying to calm her friend. "Lucy, please, there had to be another way. Murder isn't the answer."

Lucy whirled around, her eyes flashing with anger. "Isn't it? Tell me, Sarah, what other choice did I have? Divorce? He would have never let me go, not without destroying me first. How would Denny react to the news that you don't think murder is the answer? Oh wait, we can't ask him. He's currently being eaten by a thousand fish. You're not in any position to judge me, sweetheart."

She stepped closer to Sarah, her voice dropping to a whisper. "You almost ruined everything; you know. Again, for me, you almost ruined fucking everything. I thought I could trust you, but now I see that even you don't understand the depths of my desperation. Some friend you turned out to be."

Sarah wondered how well she knew the woman standing before her and what other secrets lay hidden beneath the surface.

"Lucy—"

"Save it," Lucy cut her off.

"That footage is my insurance, Sarah. My freedom. You didn't think I had it in me to mastermind this whole thing, did you?" Her eyes gleamed with the kind of desperate determination that comes from having nothing left to lose.

Lucy leaned against the mahogany desk, the air of casual cruelty about her as natural as her skin.

"Edward was to nudge Graham overboard in the dead of night," Lucy confessed with a shrug, her voice a melody of malice. "Simple, really. But then you had to play the hero with Denny and mess everything up for me. You became the murderer that this voyage shouldn't have had. You spoilt my plan, darling."

"Our plans," said Edward, placing a hand on Lucy's shoulder.

Sarah noticed Lucy wince slightly as Edward touched her.

Sarah felt a searing anger rise, burning away the shock that had momentarily paralysed her. "You... you killed your own husband?"

"Killed?" Lucy scoffed, rolling her eyes. "I liberated myself. And Graham? A necessary sacrifice for my happiness. But also, one minor point: I didn't kill him; he did."

Lucy extended her arm, a slender finger pointed firmly at Edward with unwavering determination. As she gazed intently ahead, the corners of her mouth curled upwards in a knowing smile. Edward couldn't help but admire her strength and conviction. His eyes followed her gesture to an unknown destination, but all that mattered was how she commanded attention with just one simple movement. Edward was smitten.

"I would kill a thousand men if it meant being with you," Edward said, meaning every word of it.

He adjusted his cufflinks, a gesture so at odds with the gravity of his words.

As Edward mentioned being together with Lucy, Sarah saw an unmistakable look on her friend's face.

"Graham never threatened my family's business. He never even met my family. My Dad hasn't killed himself. That was a lie. I made it up so you wouldn't suspect my darling Lucy. I don't even talk to my parents. I hate them." He stopped and turned to Sarah; his gaze sharp.

"Graham's demise, however, presented a different opportunity."

"An opportunity?" Sarah repeated, her thoughts racing.

"Lucy's insurance pay out," Edward explained as if discussing the weather.

"A steady income stream to keep this ship—and my legacy—afloat. Behind all this glitz and glamour, my little ship is in trouble, and I'd do anything not to lose her. We'd do anything not to lose her. So, Graham dying presented an opportunity for both of us and meant we could be together."

"Blackmail," Sarah spat the word out like venom.

"Let's call it a mutually beneficial arrangement," Lucy interjected, her smile never wavering even as her eyes grew colder.

"Mutually beneficial?" Sarah's fists clenched at her sides. "You're monsters."

"Darling," Lucy drawled, her tone mocking, "we're survivors. Also, again, I'd like to point out that I'm the one in a room with two murderers; I should be terrified." Lucy laughed mockingly in Sarah's direction.

"Terri's hoody?" Sarah's voice faltered, the words catching in her throat. "You planted it?"

"Of course," Lucy said with a shrug. "It was simple, really. A splash of red here, a shred of doubt there."

Edward leaned against the mahogany desk, his fingers drumming a silent rhythm. The room felt smaller, as if the air was strangling her.

"Simple?" Sarah's mind reeled, images flashing before her—Terri's tearful confusion, the trust they shared. How could she have been so blind?

"You tried to frame an innocent woman."

"Again, collateral damage," Lucy replied, the term slipping off her tongue like a seasoned gambler laying down a winning hand.

"She'll bounce back. She's better without him."

"Will she?" Sarah took a step forward, the need for justice burning within her.

"How can you be so callous? She's okay now, but she could have been found guilty.

You could have watched her go to prison."

"Survival, my dear. We needed thinking time," Edward interjected with a smoothness that belied the sharpness of his gaze.

"It's all about survival."

"By destroying others?" Sarah challenged, her survival instincts kicking in. She couldn't let fear paralyse her—not now. Not when so much was at stake.

"Isn't that what life is all about? Also, you helped to kill Graham to save yourself; you're a hypocrite." Lucy's taunt dared Sarah to disagree.

"You won't get away with this." Sarah said quietly.

Lucy's laughter was a cold melody, out of tune with the gravity of the situation.

"Oh, Sarah, we go down, you go down," she said, her eyes glinting with something dark and unfathomable.

"Always the idealist, but you're as bad as us, Sarah; you're with us now. You're a murderer!"

"I didn't murder Denny for gain. It was justice, passion."

Sarah shot back, her resolve hardening.

"You're right. Murder is such an ugly word," Lucy countered.

"Ugly but fitting," Sarah retorted. There had to be a way out to expose them without endangering herself further. She just needed time.

"Enough of this," Edward said, his voice a command that sliced through the charged air.

"We have business to attend to."

"Indeed," Lucy agreed, turning her back on Sarah, dismissing her presence as if she were nothing more than an inconvenient shadow. She placed her hand on Edward's shoulder, and Sarah had a fleeting thought that the touch seemed over-familiar, as if they were comfortable in ways that Sarah hadn't seen before. They had been pretending not to know each other for the whole journey.

As they conspired in their silk-wrapped deceit, Sarah watched them, every sense heightened. She was in their domain, unarmed and outnumbered, but she was far from defeated.

"Game on," she whispered to herself, the words barely audible.

But it was enough. Enough to steel her spine, to push her forward into the murky depths of the unknown.

"Fine," Sarah conceded, the word cutting through her clenched teeth like glass.

"I'll help with the payments." Her mind churned with calculations. She needed a way to turn the tables.

"Smart choice, but we're not talking about twenty pounds here and there; you can sell your house; I'm talking about that kind of money," Lucy said, the corners of her lips curving into a smirk.

"But don't think for a second you can outsmart me, darling."

Sarah's nod was almost imperceptible, a subtle bow in a dangerous game. She watched Edward's eyes, searching for a fissure in his veneer of confidence, but found none. They were playing for keeps, and she was far from holding any real power.

"Speaking of smart moves," Lucy continued, pacing the room like a caged lioness readying for the hunt, "The hoody? Oh, it was perfect—some chatter about a figure in a red hoody seen that night.

We know whoever was wearing that hoody, a random passenger, had nothing to do with this. But the stupid ship's security latched onto it. So, I took one from the store on board, with gloves on, of course, and slipped it into Terri's wardrobe while everyone was busy wringing their hands over Denny's unfortunate accident."

"You wore gloves? As if my stupid security team could look at DNA," Edward laughed.

"They let everyone on board touch it before it gets to any authorities."

Lucy laughed, "Yeah, good point."

Lucy's casual voice and her toying with the lives she'd upended sparked a fury deep within Sarah, a burning desire for justice that refused to be quenched.

Lucy stopped and turned to face Sarah.

"Let's call it... liberation. From a life that never suited me. From a husband who thought he owned me. I'm free now, I'm free, and with dear Edward's help, I'll stay that way."

"Of course," Sarah forced a smile. She met Lucy's cold stare with one of her own.

"Anything to keep you happy, Lucy."

"Good girl," Lucy purred and turned back to Edward.

"So, Sarah, we'll keep the hard drive, and you just need to make some regular payments. That's it. We can discuss the numbers later."

"But you know Peter and I can't afford it." Sarah pleaded.

"Oh, I'm sure you'll work it out; like I said, you must nearly own your house now, and you don't need such a nice car," Lucy smiled.

As Sarah hurriedly left the room, her breath moved with fear and anger. She couldn't shake off the feeling of being trapped. This was new to her, and she didn't know how to handle it. Her mind was torn between wanting to run away and wanting to confront the situation head-on. But at this moment, she felt utterly helpless.

Her hands shook as she clutched at the fabric of her skirt, the soft material offering no comfort for the dread that clawed at her insides.

She reached her cabin, pushed open the door, and leaned against it, closing her eyes to steady her breathing. The confined cabin was filled with the echo of Lucy's smug revelations and Edward's calculated manoeuvres. Sarah could still hear Lucy's malice and the gleam of triumph in her eyes.

"Think, Sarah, think," she muttered to herself. She paced the small room. She had to find a way out of this web they'd woven around her, but how? Every scenario she conjured up ended with her being trapped further into their vile plot.

Peter was asleep, but started to stir.

"Where's the evidence?" she whispered, her gaze darting around the room as if the walls might whisper an answer. But there was nothing.

Her thoughts raced back to Edward's study, to the hard drive that held power over them all.

"If only I could get my hands on it," she breathed, the idea sparking a desperate glimmer of hope. The risk was immense, but the reward was worth her life.

But Sarah had another feeling she had felt in only her darkest times; this felt like the end of the road for her. She hated nothing more than being trapped; this time, it felt like there was no way out. She would never truly be safe, and while that hard drive existed, she was seconds away from her life, completely changing. She'd had enough, and she knew she couldn't live with her and Peter having to sell their house. And even then, would Lucy's demands stop?

It felt like there was only one way out, and she knew it.

CHAPTER TWENTY-THREE

WEDNESDAY MORNING
THE EMERALD EMPRESS
DAY FIVE OF THE CRUISE

Sarah's hands trembled as she fumbled with the latch on the cabin door. The metal was slick, and nervous sweat coated her palms. She needed air and to think, but she also felt like there was no way out.

"Sarah? Where are you going?" Peter's voice was laced with concern. He sat up in bed, the sheets rustling softly.

"I just need some air. To clear my head." Sarah's voice sounded distant, even to her ears.

Peter swung his legs over the side of the bed and stood.

"It's pouring rain out there. You'll catch a cold." He reached for her, but she stepped back to avoid his touch.

"I'll only be a few minutes." She forced a tight smile. "Don't worry about me. I'll be fine."

Peter's brow furrowed, but he nodded slowly. “Alright. But I'll be here when you get back. If you need to talk...”

Sarah's throat constricted. She gave a jerky nod and pulled open the door. Cool, damp air rushed in, chilling her flushed skin.

“I know. Thank you. I love you.”

Sarah knew that sounded too much like what it was, a goodbye forever, she knew this would be the last time she would see her husband.

She stepped out into the narrow hallway, pulling the door shut behind her with a soft click. Her breath came in short gasps as she hurried down the corridor. She needed to leave this world to escape the suffocating guilt that threatened to consume her. She knew this was the end of the road. She was in too deep.

Sarah burst through the door leading to the deck, the icy rain stinging her face and soaking through her thin clothes in seconds. She gasped, the shock of the cold making her feel alive for the first time in days.

What have I done? The thought pounded through her head. She stumbled forward, gripping the slick railing with numb fingers.

The churning black water below seemed to call to her, promising oblivion, an end to her suffering.

She knew what she needed to do to end this: join Denny and Graham. The situation had finally overtaken her, and there was no way out.

Since childhood, she had always wondered how her life would end, and now she knew, in the icy water of the North Sea, there was a comfort in the control she had over that.

Sarah closed her eyes, tilting her face up to the weeping sky. The rain mingled with the hot tears coursing down her cheeks.

She took a shuddering breath and opened her eyes.

She knew what she was going to do.

The light was impenetrable, the ocean and sky bleeding together in a grey void.

Sarah leaned forward, her hands slipping on the wet railing. She would keep leaning until her weight shifted, and it would all be over. The wind whipped her hair across her face, stinging her eyes. She could do it. Just one more step, and it would all be over. The guilt, the fear, the suffocating control Lucy and Edward held over her. Freedom was within reach.

After killing Denny, there was a part of her that knew it would end this way.

Living with the knowledge of what she'd done would always be too much; she would be the third casualty of the Emerald Empress on this trip.

She leaned even more.

The wind whistled past her face. Knowing it was only seconds, she started to shift her weight over the side of the ship.

"Sarah! What are you doing?" Terri's panicked voice cut through the howling wind.

Sarah froze, instinctively grabbing the railing. She turned slowly, blinking the rain from her eyes. Terri stood a few feet away, her eyes wide with alarm.

"Stay back," Sarah warned, her voice raw and trembling. "Please, just let me go."

Terri edged closer; her hands held out in a placating gesture.

"Sarah, whatever it is, we can talk about it. Just step away from the edge."

Sarah shook her head, a mirthless laugh escaping her lips.

"You don't understand. There's no coming back from what I've done. I'm trapped, and this is the only way out."

"That's not true," Terri insisted, her voice firm despite the fear in her eyes.

"There's always another way. You're not alone in this, Sarah. Let me help you."

"How did you find me?" Sarah shouted.

"Peter told me you'd gone for a walk, and I saw it in your eyes earlier. Sarah, there is always a way out."

Sarah hesitated, torn between the allure of escape and the glimmer of hope in Terri's words. She looked back at the churning water, then at Terri's outstretched hand. She knew that if she did it now, Terri would have to witness it, and she didn't want her to have to deal with that.

"I'm scared," she whispered, her voice barely audible over the wind.

Terri took another step forward, her hand still extended.

"I know. But you don't have to face this alone. Trust me, Sarah. We can find a way through this together."

Sarah's resolve wavered, her grip on the railing loosening. She wanted to believe Terri and think there was still a chance for redemption. Slowly, she reached out and took Terri's hand, allowing herself to be pulled back from the edge.

Sarah allowed Terri to guide her away from the railing, her heart still racing from the adrenaline. They found a nearby bench, sheltered from the worst of the rain, and sat down.

Terri turned to face Sarah; her green eyes filled with compassion.

"Talk to me, Sarah. What's going on?"

At first, Sarah couldn't find the words. The guilt and fear that had consumed her for so long seemed to choke her, making it impossible to speak. But as Terri waited patiently, her hand resting on Sarah's arm in support, the words began to tumble out.

"It's Denny," Sarah said, her voice trembling. "I... I killed him."

Terri's eyes widened, but she didn't pull away. Instead, she gently squeezed Sarah's arm, encouraging her to continue.

"It was an accident," Sarah rushed on, the words pouring out of her now.

"We were arguing, and things got out of hand. I didn't mean to hurt him, but..." She trailed off, the memory of that night still raw and painful. "Everything he'd done to me, Terri, it came to the front of my mind as he stood there, and I just did it in an instant.

I could see you going the same way I did; he promised me, Terri, he promised he wouldn't treat anyone else like he treated me."

"Now Lucy and Edward are using it against you," Terri guessed, her voice soft with understanding.

Sarah nodded, but with surprise, tears streaming down her face. How did Terri know that?

"They are blackmailing me; I feel like I'm suffocating, like I'll never be free of this."

Terri remained silent for a moment; her expression was thoughtful. When she spoke again, her voice was determined.

"I promise you, we'll find a way out of this; I know what it's like to feel trapped, like there's no way out." She paused, taking a deep breath before continuing.

"I was in that abusive relationship for years. I thought I had to endure it because I had nowhere else. I felt so alone and had no idea he'd done it to anyone else."

Sarah listened intently, her heart aching for Terri's pain. She could see the shadows of those dark times lingering in Terri's eyes.

Sarah felt tears prickling at the corners of her eyes.

She had been so focused on her guilt and shame that she had forgotten about the people who loved her, the ones who would stand by her no matter what. Although not close in age, these two women bonded through their dark experiences with the same man.

"You're not alone, Sarah," Terri said, as if reading her thoughts.

"You have people who care about you, who want to help you. Don't push them away."

Sarah nodded, a small smile tugging at her lips. For the first time in a long time, she felt a glimmer of hope, a sense that maybe there was a way out of the darkness that had consumed her for days.

"Thank you, Terri," she said softly, her voice filled with gratitude.

"Thank you for listening and for understanding."

Terri smiled, her eyes shining with warmth and compassion.

"That's what friends are for," she said. "We'll get through this together, one step at a time."

"Come back to my room", Terri said, holding Sarah's hand.

"Thank you," said Sarah.

The couple left the rainy deck. As they descended the steps, the breeze carried the faint scent of saltwater and pine. She could hear the birds' distant cries and the waves lapping against the ship; she hadn't heard those things on the way out to the deck. The weather had calmed, like they were passing through a momentary gap in the storm. But in this tranquil moment, surrounded by nature's beauty, she couldn't bring herself to regret not ending things there.

CHAPTER TWENTY-FOUR

WEDNESDAY MORNING
THE EMERALD EMPRESS
DAY FIVE OF THE CRUISE

Terri and Sarah walked into Terri's room, their clothes drenched and their faces plastered with hair from the downpour outside. Terri quickly locked the door behind them with a click. She grabbed a plush white towel from the rack and tossed it to Sarah.

"Here, dry yourself off," Terri said, her voice unsteady. She wrung her hands anxiously as Sarah patted the towel over her soaked hair and clothes. What was she going to say? How could she even begin to have this conversation?

Sarah glanced up, noticing the tension in Terri's posture.

"You just saved my life, Terri. Thank you. Are you ok?"

"I just... a lot has happened," Terri replied vaguely, averting her gaze. She paced to the window, staring at the rain pounding against the glass.

Sarah watched her friend with growing concern, the damp towel hanging forgotten in her hands. "Terri, you know you can talk to me about anything, right? I'm here for you."

Terri nodded, biting her lower lip. She took a deep breath and turned to face Sarah. It was now or never.

"Sarah, there's something I need to tell you..."

Terri's voice trembled slightly as she spoke.

"I already knew what happened to Denny. I saw you on the deck that night, Sarah. I saw everything."

Sarah froze; the towel slipped from her grasp, falling to the floor with a soft thud. She struggled to find her voice, her mind reeling with the implications of Terri's revelation.

"What... what are you saying?"

"I followed Denny that night; I was worried he'd get into a fight with someone and embarrass everyone," Terri confessed, her eyes locked on Sarah's face.

"I saw the confrontation. And then... Sarah, it looked like you were defending yourself. He was blind drunk and probably would have fallen on his own." She swallowed hard; the memory was still vivid in her mind.

"But I did see you push him over the railing. I was on the deck above you, looking down."

"I don't understand," Sarah managed to say, her voice barely above a whisper.

"If you saw what happened, why didn't you report it to security? Why didn't you tell anyone? They locked you up!"

Terri sighed, running a hand through her damp hair.

"Because I empathise with you, Sarah. I know the pain and suffering Denny inflicted on those around him. I couldn't bear the thought of you facing the consequences alone. You did it for all of us."

Sarah's eyes filled with tears. She had carried the burden of her actions to this point, the weight of her secret threatening to crush her. Now, amid her darkest moment, she found an unexpected ally in Terri.

"I knew I would be proven innocent; there were so many cameras that would have seen me in a different place," Terri whispered.

Sarah nodded, her vision blurring as the tears spilt down her cheeks.

Sarah wiped her tears, her voice trembling as she began to speak.

"It wasn't just about me, Terri. It was about all of us and how Denny treated everyone around him. I couldn't let him continue to hurt the people I cared about, especially you."

"I know, Sarah. I see the pain he caused and the fear he instilled in all of us. With him gone, I feel like I can finally breathe again. It's a twisted consolation, but the life insurance money will give me a chance to start over, to build a life free from his torment. I don't even need to check the policy; I know he was covered entirely; he always insisted on it when he went climbing in the Alps, all kinds of accidental death, whatever he was doing."

Sarah reached out, grasping Terri's hand in a gesture of solidarity.

"You deserve that chance, Terri. You deserve to be free from his shadow, to find happiness on your terms."

Taking a deep breath, she told Terri everything, unravelling the tangled web of deceit that had led to that fateful night. She spoke of Lucy and Edward, of their plot to frame Terri for Denny's murder, of the red hoody planted in Terri's wardrobe as false evidence to frame her.

Terri listened intently; her brow furrowed as the pieces fell into place. The betrayal of those she had considered friends cut deep, but the truth of Sarah's words rang clear. They had all been pawns in a game of manipulation and greed, their lives forever changed by the actions of a few.

But then Terri's eyes flickered with a sudden realisation. She hesitated momentarily, her fingers fidgeting with the edge of the towel draped around her shoulders.

"Wait, there's something else," she said, her voice louder than it had been.

Sarah leaned forward; her curiosity was piqued by the intensity in Terri's gaze.

"What is it, Terri? Whatever it is, you can trust me."

Terri stood abruptly, crossing the room to her dresser. With trembling hands, she reached for a simple wooden picture frame.

In happier times, the image of a smiling couple, Terri and Denny, was visible beneath the glass. She turned back to Sarah, holding the frame close to her chest.

"I bought this with me," Terri began, her words catching in her throat.

"It's a spy camera picture frame. I wanted to gather evidence of what Denny was doing to me, the violence, to have proof if I needed it. My friend suggested it to me; I didn't know what I would do with the footage; just collecting some evidence was step one. She set it up for me. It just records when there's movement in front of it. She said it would help if I needed it. I don't know how it works or even if it is working. "

Sarah's eyes widened in surprise, her mind racing with the implications of Terri's revelation.

"A spy camera? But... have you looked at the footage yet?"

Terri shook her head, a flicker of fear crossing her features.

"No, I don't have anything I can watch it on. If anything happened, I would give it back to my friend to get the footage from it for me. I also couldn't risk him finding out."

She paused, her gaze dropping to the frame in her hands.

"But now... now I wonder if it might have captured something important. You said Lucy was in here?"

Sarah rose from her seat, crossing the room to stand beside Terri. She placed a comforting hand on her friend's shoulder, feeling the tension thrumming beneath her fingertips.

"If there's footage on that camera, Terri, we must see it. It could be the key to unravelling this whole twisted mess."

Terri nodded, a newfound determination settling over her features.

Sarah pulled out her phone, her fingers flying across the screen as she composed a message to Peter.

"I'm asking Peter to bring his laptop over. He always brings it on our trips, always convinced he'll 'get some work done', but never does. We need to see what's on that camera."

Terri nodded, her grip tightening on the picture frame.

"You're not alone, Terri. We're in this together, no matter what." She glanced at her phone, watching Peter's reply appear on the screen.

"He's on his way. We'll get to the bottom of this, I promise."

Minutes later, a soft knock echoed through the room. Sarah hurried to the door, opening it to reveal Peter's concerned face.

"I came as quickly as I could. What's going on?"

Sarah ushered him inside, locking the door behind them.

"Terri has a spy camera hidden in a picture frame. We think it might have captured something important."

"A spy camera? That's... that's incredible. Let me see if I can access the footage." He set his laptop on the desk, his fingers flying across the keyboard as he worked to establish a connection.

Sarah and Terri huddled behind him, their hearts pounding in unison as they waited for the footage to load. The room was silent except for the soft hum of the laptop fan.

As the screen flickered to life, Sarah held her breath, her eyes fixed on the grainy image.

She knew that the next few moments could change their lives forever, that the truth they uncovered might be more helpful than they ever imagined.

Terri watched as screenshots of the videos appeared, one file for each time the frame had captured movement.

Terri's gaze drifted to a snapshot of Denny, frozen from an earlier moment on their trip.

She couldn't help but feel a sense of emptiness, even though she wouldn't bring him back if she could. But perhaps it was a good thing, a test of sorts to gauge her true feelings for him.

She felt nothing.

"That one!" Sarah pointed to one of the last images captured.

The video began to play, and they watched with bated breath as a figure entered Terri's room. As the image sharpened, Sarah's eyes widened in disbelief.

"Is that... Lucy?" she whispered, her voice trembling.

Terri nodded; her jaw clenched tight.

"It is. I can't believe she would do something like this."

On the screen, Lucy acted purposefully, her movements quick and slippery as she made her way to Terri's wardrobe. She reached inside a bag, pulled out the familiar red hoody, and placed it in the wardrobe—the same one that had been seen on someone on the night of Denny's murder. Although Lucy's actions were strange, there was no doubt it was her as she looked directly at the camera, probably looking at the picture of Denny and Terri in the frame.

The implications of what they saw hit her like a freight train, and she struggled to catch her breath.

"She was trying to frame you," Sarah whispered, her voice barely audible.

"She wants the police to think you killed Denny."

Terri's eyes were fixed on the screen, her expression a mix of shock and fury.

"I can't believe it. I trusted her. I thought she was my friend. We had a….." Terri realised she'd said too much.

As the video ended, Sarah and Terri exchanged a knowing glance. They knew this footage was more than just evidence; it was a weapon they could use to protect themselves and expose the truth.

Sarah also needed clarification. Why would Lucy want to frame Terri if she knew Sarah was guilty?

Why not just let everyone think it was an accident?

Why not just report Sarah?

Sarah's mind raced with possibilities, knowing they now held the power to expose Lucy and Edward's lies.

They were now in the driving seat.

"We have to confront them," Sarah said, her voice steady.

"We have to make them pay for what they're trying to do."

Terri nodded, her expression hardening with resolve.

"Together," she said, reaching out to take Sarah's hand. "We'll face them together."

Peter stepped forward; his laptop clutched tightly in his hands.

"I'm with you," he said, his voice wavering slightly, knowing he was the least brave of all three of them. "Whatever happens, we're in this together. I've saved copies of the video on my laptop and this thumb drive."

Sarah felt a surge of gratitude for her friends' unwavering support in the face of such adversity.

Sarah pulled out her phone and added Lucy and Edward to a message chat.

```
Text message:
We need to meet you. Things have changed. I'll come to Edward's suite in 15 minutes. Both of you will need to be there.
```

The message displayed two ticks, indicating both Edward and Lucy had read it.

"Let's do this," Sarah said to Terri and Peter.

CHAPTER TWENTY-FIVE

WEDNESDAY MORNING

THE EMERALD EMPRESS

DAY FIVE OF THE CRUISE

Sarah's hand trembled as she reached out and rapped sharply on the door to Edward's suite. Terri and Peter stood close behind her. Peter clutched his laptop as if his life depended on it. After a long moment, the door swung open.

"Sarah," Edward said smoothly, his face an unreadable mask.

"Please, come in." His eyes flicked to Terri and Peter.

"All of you."

They stepped into the opulent room. Lucy was perched on the edge of a velvet settee, her hands clasped primly in her lap. Sarah noticed how her friend looked nervous.

"We need to talk," Sarah said, her voice steady. She pulled the spy camera frame from Terri.

Edward arched an eyebrow.

"I'm not sure I follow."

Ignoring him, Sarah turned to Lucy.

"The footage shows you planting a red hoody in Denny's room after he was killed."

Lucy paled, her mouth falling open. Edward stepped forward, placing a hand on Lucy's shoulder.

"Let's all calm down," he said.

"Lucy wouldn't have planted that hoody?" Edward's eyes looked expectantly at Lucy. He knew she had, and they had admitted it to Sarah, but he wanted to deny it in front of Terri and Peter.

"We have video evidence of what Lucy did," Terri cut in.

Sarah nodded.

"Why, Lucy? Why would you try to frame Terri? When you knew it was me?"

Lucy looked up at Edward, her expression pleading. He gave a subtle shake of his head.

"I... I don't know what you're talking about," Lucy stammered.

"This is ridiculous." She glanced at Edward, desperately not wanting to be the reason everything was failing.

Peter spoke up, his usually gentle voice stiff with anger.

"Stop lying, Lucy. We all saw the video. Just tell us the truth."

Peter spun around the sleek laptop and clicked play on the video. The screen flickered to life and projected a few seconds of footage, enough to confirm the validity of their words.

The air crackled with tension as everyone stared at Lucy, waiting. Sarah held her breath.

After a long moment, Lucy buried her face in her hands and let out a choked sob. She looked at Edward.

"I'm sorry," she whispered. "I'm so sorry."

Relief and sadness warred within Sarah. The truth was finally coming out.

CHAPTER TWENTY-SIX

WEDNESDAY MORNING
THE EMERALD EMPRESS
DAY FIVE OF THE CRUISE

"But why, Lucy? If you knew I was the one who..." She couldn't bring herself to say the words out loud.

"Why would you try to frame Terri?"

Lucy lifted her head, tears streaking her face, and her mascara started to run. Her eyes moved to Edward as if seeking permission to speak. Edward gave a curt nod.

"I did it to protect you, Sarah," Lucy whispered, her voice trembling.

Sarah's brow furrowed.

"Protect me? I don't understand..."

Lucy stood with her posture tense and defensive. Edward leaned against his desk, waiting for her to speak.

"You did that... for me?" Sarah whispered; her voice choked with emotion.

Lucy nodded, fresh tears spilling down her cheeks. "I couldn't let them find out it was you, Sarah. I couldn't let it destroy your life. I knew what he put you through, and I understood. I needed to save you. I'm so sorry, Terri. I knew they wouldn't come after you if they thought Terri did it. I didn't think it through; I just did it. We had a plan; you messed it up, but I didn't want you to get into trouble. I knew I could make Edward bury the footage, but if Terri were under suspicion, you wouldn't be. I love you, Sarah."

Terri nodded as if she understood. She knew she was listening to the confession of a desperate woman protecting a friend, and Terri knew she would have done the same thing.

Sarah couldn't believe what she was hearing. Even amid this nightmare, Lucy had been looking out for her. She reached out and pulled Lucy into a tight embrace, feeling the other woman's body shake with sobs.

"Thank you," Sarah whispered, her tears falling freely. "Thank you for being my friend."

As they clung to each other, Sarah's mind raced with new questions. What hold did Edward have over Lucy? And how far would he go to protect his interests?

Terri watched Sarah and Lucy's heart-wrenching exchange with tears in her eyes. Her heart ached with empathy as she watched their emotions spill over into each other.

“We're in this together,” Terri whispered, her voice fierce with determination.

“I understand why you did it, Lucy,” Terri said sincerely in her direction, “I would have done the same thing for my friend.”

The three women stood there momentarily, drawing strength from each other. But the sound of a desk drawer slamming shut shattered the moment.

They turned to see Edward standing by his desk, a cold fury etched on his face. In their moment of reconciliation, they had failed to watch Edward’s movements. In his hand, he held a gleaming silver pistol.

“How touching,” he sneered, his voice dripping with sarcasm.

“But I'm afraid your little reunion is over.”

“Edward, please,” Lucy began, her voice shaking. “You don't have to do this.”

But Edward merely laughed, a harsh, bitter sound.

“Oh, but I do, my dear,” he said, his eyes glinting with malice.

"You see, I've worked too hard to build my empire to let you bring it all crashing down. Oh, and is it a good time to mention our plans for the future, Lucy?"

"Edward and I plan to be together." Lucy said, looking down.

Not in sight of Edward, Lucy winked at Sarah—a look between friends that conveyed a thousand thoughts.

Edward gestured with the gun towards the balcony. "Now, if you'll all be so kind as to step outside. Let's bring an end to all of this."

Sarah exchanged desperate glances with Lucy, Terri, and Peter. They had no choice but to comply. Slowly, they made their way towards the balcony, the cool afternoon air hitting their faces as they stepped outside.

Edward followed close behind, the gun never wavering from its aim. Sarah knew they were trapped as he shut the balcony door behind them.

The balcony had three sides and appeared to dangle over the water. The clever ship's architect had engineered it so the passengers couldn't see any part of the ship under it, only water.

A black torrent rushed underneath on three sides, and Edward stood before the door. Sarah's mind raced, searching for a way out of this almost impossible situation. She glanced at Lucy and Terri, their faces etched with fear and uncertainty. Peter was genuinely scared and knew he needed to clutch onto his laptop, which was the only evidence they had against Lucy and Edward.

Edward paced back and forth; his grip tight on the gun.

“I have to admit, I underestimated you all,” he said, his tone dripping with condescension.

“But now it's time to face the consequences of spoiling our plans.”

Sarah stepped forward; her hands raised in a placating gesture.

“Edward, listen to me,” she pleaded, her voice steady despite the terror coursing through her veins.

“We can find a way out of this that doesn't involve anyone else dying. There’s something we can do, and we all get to move on.”

He scoffed, shaking his head.

“Why should I listen to you? You've been an inconvenience since you stepped onto this bloody ship.”

Sarah took a deep breath, her mind working overtime. She knew she had to appeal to Edward's self-interest if they had any hope of survival.

"Because we have a common goal," she said, her words measured and careful.

"We all want to protect ourselves and the people we care about. What about your future with Lucy?"

"Sarah, don't," cried Peter as Sarah moved closer to Edward with her hands raised.

Edward's hands were shaking, but he didn't interrupt. He pointed the gun at Sarah's head.

Sarah pressed on, seizing the opportunity.

"Think about it, Edward. If the truth comes out, we'll all go down. You, me, Lucy... we'll all lose everything we've worked so hard for. What about your future with Lucy?"

She could see the gears turning in his head, the realisation dawning on his face. Sarah knew she had to strike while the iron was hot. His hands were shaking as he still pointed the gun at her head.

"I need to think!" Edward shouted, losing his composure.

"But if we work together, if we stick to the story that Graham killed Denny and then took his own life, we can all walk away from this unscathed. We just all need to stick to the story."

The silence stretched on, the only sound the distant crashing of waves against the ship. Finally, Edward lowered the gun, his shoulders slumping in defeat.

"What's to stop you from turning on me the moment we're off this balcony?" he asked, his voice tinged with suspicion.

Sarah met his eyes head-on, her resolve unwavering.

"Because we're all in this together now. We sink or swim together."

She could feel Lucy and Terri's eyes on her, the weight of their trust and their lives resting on her shoulders. Sarah knew she had to be strong, for all of their sakes.

"Think about it, Edward; we throw that laptop, the frame, and your CCTV hard drive over the side, and we are the only people who know the truth."

She could see the recognition on Edward's face that this was a good plan.

"So, what's it going to be?" she asked. "Do we work together and survive? Or do we tear each other apart and lose everything?"

Edward stood there in a moment of defeat and lowered the gun. He slumped, looking at the floor. As if suddenly shocked into action, Edward lurched forward and held the gun against Peter's head.

"No, Sarah, I'm done with these games; you've fucked around with me too much."

Peter closed his eyes, wondering whether he would hear the gun's bang or if it would be instant.

He knew he wasn't brave enough to do anything and would accept his fate.

"I think it'd be fair if all three of you had lost your husbands; let's see if you still feel the same then Sarah,"

"Edward…." Sarah knew she couldn't scream, couldn't shout. Any lurching could trigger Edward to fire, and the gun was resting on Peter's head.

"I love you," Peter mouthed the words towards Sarah.

"Edward, calm down. You can only make this worse." Lucy said, "Darling, lower the gun."

Lucy's voice had cut to Edward's core.

"If you kill Peter, we won't be able to be together. If we follow Sarah's plan, our dreams of being together will remain alive."

Sarah could practically see the scales tipping in his head, the balance between self-preservation and vengeance. He lowered the gun and stepped slowly backwards. Lucy had more control over Edward than anyone knew.

"The hard drive, the laptop and the photo frame," he held out his hand, his voice low and measured. "They're the only physical evidence tying us to this mess. Without them, it's just our word against two dead men."

Sarah nodded, relief flooding through her. "Exactly. We throw them overboard, and the only thing left is the message from Graham's phone to Lucy's. A message that proves he was the one behind it all."

She turned to Lucy and Terri, their faces pale in the cold light.

"Are we all in agreement? We do this together, and we never speak of it again."

Lucy swallowed hard, her eyes glistening with unshed tears. "I'm in," she whispered, her voice trembling.

Terri nodded; her jaw set with determination. "Let's do it. Let's end this nightmare once and for all."

Sarah turned back to Edward; her hand outstretched.

"The hard drive, Edward. It's time to let them go. Peter, sorry, the laptop and the picture frame."

For a moment, he hesitated, his grip tightening on the gun. Sarah's heart skipped a beat. But then, with a sigh of resignation, Edward stepped inside, and reappeared with the CCTV Hard drive.

Together, they walked to the balcony's edge, the wind whipping at their hair and clothes. Sarah looked down at the churning waters below, the black depths waiting to swallow their secrets whole. With a deep breath, they let go, watching as the hard drive, the picture frame, and laptop disappeared into the inky darkness, sinking beneath the waves and out of sight.

"Someone's buying me a new laptop," said Peter.

"Not now, Peter, bloody hell," said Lucy, without a smile.

It was done. The evidence was gone, and with it, any chance of the truth coming to light. Sarah knew they would have to live with the guilt and knowledge of what they had done for the rest of their lives.

As far as the world knew, Graham had killed Denny, then killed himself through guilt. The motive? Everyone around them had witnessed a lifetime of rivalry and torment, and it wouldn't be hard to believe.

The remaining four friends stood there, along with Edward.

"Ok, so it's simple," Lucy said. "We were all in our rooms when Denny went missing except Graham, who I can say went out for a walk; then I can tell them that Graham seemed preoccupied the day he went missing, like something was bothering him, you can all say that. We don't allude to any of our problems; just keep it simple. Really play up the rivalry Denny and Graham had."

The group, all looking down, nodded.

"You," Lucy continued, pointing to Edward, "just tell them the security cameras didn't work; there's normally no need for them on these trips."

Again, the group nodded and turned to leave the room.

But as Sarah turned to face the others, she knew they would bear the burden together.

They just now needed to stay united when questioned. Going into something like that with people they didn't trust was unnerving, but they had no choice; they would have to hope that everyone stuck to their stories. Graham pushed Denny into a fit of rage; he couldn't live with the guilt and jumped himself.

CHAPTER TWENTY-SEVEN

WEDNESDAY AFTERNOON
THE EMERALD EMPRESS
DAY FIVE OF THE CRUISE

Terri, Sarah, and Peter filed out of Edward's suite, leaving Edward and Lucy silently in the room.

Terri walked beside Sarah, her face pale and drawn. "Do you think they'll believe us?" she whispered, her voice trembling.

Sarah swallowed hard, forcing herself to nod. "They have to. It's the only story that makes sense. The bloody truth doesn't!"

Terri forced a smile.

They returned to their cabins, each lost in their thoughts. Sarah's hands shook as she unlocked her door, the day's events replaying in her mind like a nightmare she couldn't escape. They were almost there, almost off the Emerald Empress forever. Peter just sat on the sofa in their room, and Sarah imagined he was going through the story he would tell the police; she knew she would find it easier to deceive them than Peter would.

She had barely settled into her chair when a knock at the door startled her. Sarah couldn't even imagine what would be next. She opened the door to find two police officers standing outside, their faces grim; there was a different weight to these uniformed officers, much more so than the security officers on the ship.

As they made their way towards the bustling port of Southampton, a group of stern-faced police officers had boarded the ship, determined to question every person involved in the recent incident before docking; that way, they could control everyone's movements and gain all the information they needed. Their presence loomed over the passengers and crew, causing an uneasy tension to settle over the once lively atmosphere. People whispered and cast nervous glances at one another, wondering what could have warranted such intense scrutiny from the authorities. Their heavy boots echoed through the narrow corridors as they went about their enquiries. They knew from the ship's location they were still a few hours from docking.

"Sarah Emerson?" one of them asked, looking down at his passenger list.

Sarah nodded; her mouth was dry.

"Yes, that's me."

"We need you to come with us for questioning. It's about the disappearance of Denny Blackwood and Graham Winslow. Mr. Emerson, please go with my colleague. Are you both happy to do so?"

The officer gestured to a much younger officer standing next to him.

"Of course, anything we can do to help," replied Sarah.

Sarah couldn't help but think the more experienced officer would question her, leading her to believe they knew something.

Sarah's stomach churned as she followed them out of the room. She was led to a small, sterile meeting room, where she was left alone with her thoughts and the weight of the lie she was about to tell. She imagined the room was used for some of the more corporate events that sometimes happened on the ship while it was docked.

Minutes ticked by, each one feeling like an eternity. Finally, the door opened, and the detective entered, his face lined with weariness. He was accompanied by someone else, and Sarah assumed they needed to interview in pairs.

"Mrs. Emerson," he began, settling into the chair across from her.

"Can you tell me what happened the night that Denny Blackwood disappeared?"

Sarah took a deep breath, her heart racing.

"I can't tell you much, really; we all were in high spirits as we boarded, all looking forward to the holiday. Everything was fine except the ever-present tension between Graham and Denny. We all thought that would have died away with the years, but it was worse than ever, and we were just all so worried one of them would crack."

"I see," said the first interviewer whilst the second scribbled notes frantically.

"We just all feel so guilty we didn't do something to stop it," Sarah looked down at the table.

"Well, I'm sure none of you could guess something so bad would happen."

With that comment from the interviewer, Sarah knew she was winning.

"What do you think happened that night, Mrs. Emerson?"

"It was Graham," she said, her voice trembling. "He killed Denny. Lucy has a text from Graham, confessing. They had always been at each other's throats since we met. We knew that one day, one of them would kill the other; they hated each other. We all knew the atmosphere had been building."

The interviewer leaned forward, his eyes searching her face.

"Where were you when this happened?"

"I was with Peter," Sarah lied, the words tasting bitter on her tongue.

"We were in our cabin, having drinks. We didn't know what was happening until the next morning."

The detective nodded, jotting down notes in his pocketbook.

"What about Edward Smythe? Where was he during all of this?"

Sarah swallowed hard, her palms sweating.

"I have no idea; we hardly saw him on the ship. I assume he was busy running everything," she said.

The questioning seemed to drag on forever, each new query twisting the knife of guilt more deeply into Sarah's gut. But she held fast to the story, repeating it over and over until it almost felt like the truth.

Finally, the detective closed his notebook, his face unreadable.

"Thank you, Mrs. Emerson. That will be all for now."

As she returned to her cabin, Sarah stood on shaky legs, feeling dizzy. She knew the others were being questioned, too.

Each stuck to the same story, the same lie. Unknown to Sarah, they had all repeated it perfectly, forming a story convenient for the police officers to believe.

As the ship stood still in the darkness, Sarah knew their fate was in the balance, teetering on a knife's edge.

The police interrogated each friend individually, their eyes sharp and accusatory as they searched for any inconsistencies in their stories. The fluorescent lights flickered above as the friends sat in a similar small, cold meeting rooms with hard metal chairs. Each answered the same questions over and over again, their words rehearsed and matching perfectly with each other's accounts. Sweat beaded on their foreheads as the pressure intensified, but they stood firm in their story. They had always heard that the simplest explanation was the most likely, and the lie was the most probable story.

After all the questioning had finished, the friends slowly closed the doors to their rooms for the last time, each taking one final look at the familiar surroundings before joining the others in the lobby. The ship had returned to the same part of the dock they had departed from just a few days ago, but it felt like a lifetime had passed.

As they stood together, watching as the crew secured the vessel to the dock, memories of their journey flooded their minds. They had been told to wait in the lobby for an update on the investigation and told they were free to go or they'd be taken to a local police station.

Lucy, Sarah, Peter, and Terri stood shoulder to shoulder in a tense, anticipatory silence. They could see the faint glimmer of sunlight peeking through the clouds just ahead - a symbol of the freedom that awaited them mere minutes away if things would only go their way. The four of them shared a moment, knowing they had come this far together and would soon be able to break free from their confinement. So close, but so far.

Terri, looking the most nervous of everyone, whispered, "Do you think they bought it?"

Sarah forced a smile, trying to project a confidence she didn't feel.

"Of course they did. We all stuck to the plan. There's no reason for them to suspect anything else."

But even as the words left her mouth, Sarah couldn't shake the nagging doubt that gnawed at her insides. The police had seemed satisfied with their statements, but what if they started digging deeper? What if they found some inconsistency, some crack in their carefully crafted facade? Edward was the unknown, but they knew his future hopes with Lucy would keep him on message; he wouldn't want to do anything to scupper those plans.

Footsteps echoed through the lobby, and Sarah looked up to see a uniformed officer approaching them. She braced herself for the worst.

The officer's face was impassive, betraying no hint of accusation or suspicion.

"Mrs. Emerson, Mrs. Winslow, Mr. Emerson, Mrs. Blackwood," he said, nodding to each of them.

"I have an update on our investigation."

The group held their breath and tried to look as relaxed as possible.

"Thank you all for your co-operation. We found no evidence to suggest anyone else's involvement in the disappearance of Graham Winslow or Denny Blackwood. I am truly sorry for your loss.

We have taken your details and will contact you if we need anything further, but you can leave the ship. Obviously, there will be an official inquest, but you'll be called as necessary."

A wave of relief washed over Sarah, so intense she thought she might faint. Beside her, Lucy let out a shaky breath, and Peter's shoulders sagged as the tension drained from his body.

"Thank you, officer," Sarah managed to say, her voice barely above a whisper.

"So... we're free to go?"

The officer nodded. "Yes, you're all free to go. The ship will be docking at the port shortly. You can disembark whenever you're ready; we have your details."

As the officer walked away, Sarah felt a strange mixture of emotions. Relief, yes, but also guilt and a sense of unease that she couldn't quite shake. She wanted to get off the Emerald Empress and never see it again.

CHAPTER TWENTY-EIGHT

WEDNESDAY EVENING
THE EMERALD EMPRESS
DAY FIVE OF THE CRUISE

Terri stepped onto the deck, the salty sea air filling her lungs. She glanced at Sarah and Peter beside her, their faces etched with the same relief and unease she felt coursing through her. The nightmare was over; the scars remained, but a new life awaited her.

Lucy approached them, her blonde hair whipping in the wind. She first pulled Terri into a tight embrace, holding on a moment longer than necessary. Terri stiffened slightly, as the complicated history between them affected her body, but she appreciated the sentiment.

"I'm so glad you're okay," Lucy whispered. Then she turned to hug Sarah and Peter.

"What a mess, huh? I still can't believe it."

Sarah nodded; her eyes distant.

"It doesn't feel real. I keep expecting to wake up and find out it was all a bad dream."

"I know what you mean," Peter said grimly. His hand found Sarah's and squeezed.

Lucy glanced back towards the ship.

"Listen, I need to speak to Edward before we dock. But I wanted to see you all first." She paused, seeming to search for the right words.

"After everything... I want you to know how much your friendship means to me."

Terri shifted uncomfortably, avoiding Lucy's eyes. The secrets they shared would never leave her. She forced a tight smile.

"Thanks, Lucy. Let's all move on."

Lucy returned the smile, a flicker of understanding passing between them.

Terri released a shaky breath she didn't realise she'd been holding. It was over, she told herself firmly—time to leave the darkness behind and start anew. But even as the thought formed, doubt crept in like a chill.

Lucy took a few steps from the group to look over the side and investigate what was happening on the dock. Terri felt a sudden urge to follow her. She turned to Sarah and Peter, her voice apologetic. "I'll be right back. There's something I need to say to Lucy."

"Of course. We'll wait for you here." Sarah said with concern, but she nodded.

Terri hurried after Lucy, not sure what she was going to say. She caught up to her just as Lucy reached the ship's railing.

"Lucy, wait."

Lucy turned, surprise flickering across her face. "Terri? What is it?"

Terri glanced around, ensuring they were alone. She took a deep breath, steeling herself.

"I just wanted to thank you. For not saying anything about... about my involvement."

Lucy's expression softened. She reached out, laying a gentle hand on Terri's arm.

"Of course. We all did what we had to do. It's not my place to judge. Things worked out as we wanted, just in the wrong order. Sarah will interfere, won't she?"

Terri felt tears prick at the corners of her eyes, but couldn't bring herself to smile at Lucy's joke. Determined to maintain her composure, she blinked them back.

"Still. I know it couldn't have been easy for you. Keeping all these secrets. I understand you want to save Sarah; everyone needs a friend like you."

A shadow passed over Lucy's face, gone as quickly as it appeared. She smiled.

"We all have our secrets, Terri. Some are just bigger than others. You are where you need to be. What's happened is what needed to happen."

Terri nodded. She understood all too well the secrets they carried—the things they had done, the lies they had told. These secrets bound them together in a way that could never be undone.

Lucy squeezed Terri's arm, her touch reassuring. "It's time to let go of the past. To move forward. For all of us."

Terri managed a small smile.

"You're right. Thank you, Lucy. For everything."

They shared a long look, a silent acknowledgement of all that had transpired between them. Lucy walked back over towards Sarah and Peter, leaving Terri in a dream.

Terri stood there momentarily, watching the space where Lucy had been. She felt a strange mix of relief, gratitude, and a lingering sense of unease. But there was also a glimmer of hope. Hope for a future free from the shadows of the past.

With a deep breath, Terri turned and returned to Sarah and Peter. It was time to start anew.

As Terri walked down the walkway to the dock, Sarah shouted, “Good luck, Terri!”

Her voice carried a mix of warmth and melancholy. Terri paused, catching Sarah's eyes. She saw the understanding in her friend's eyes, the unspoken acknowledgement of all they had been through together. Terri smiled a genuine smile this time and waved.

“Thanks you. Take care of yourself.”

Sarah nodded; her smile tinged with sadness. They both knew that their paths were diverging and that the future held different journeys for each of them. They were sure they'd never see each other again; Denny had been their only connection. They also knew they wanted to leave the past few days behind.

“We're free,” Lucy whispered.

Peter hugged Lucy, then pulled in Sarah, his arms encircling both women.

As they pulled apart, Lucy's eyes shone with a newfound determination. She looked at Sarah and Peter. “We've been given a second chance. A chance to start over, to build a new life.”

Sarah nodded, feeling a surge of resolve. She glanced at Peter, seeing the same determination mirrored in his eyes. They had each other, and together, they would face whatever challenges lay ahead.

With a final look at the ship, Sarah and Peter turned away, hand in hand.

As they moved towards the dock, Sarah paused, a thought niggling at the back of her mind. She turned back to Lucy, who was walking a few steps behind them.

"Lucy," Sarah said, her voice laced with curiosity, "What about you? What are you going to do now? What was all that stuff with you and Edward having a future together? Will I see you again?"

Lucy slowed her steps, and a mysterious smile played on her lips. She looked at Sarah, her blue eyes glinting with an unreadable emotion.

"You'll never see me again," she said, her voice soft but firm.

Sarah knew that she meant it.

"What do you mean?" she asked, her grip on Peter's hand tightening.

Lucy shook her head, her smile widening.

"It's better this way," she said, her tone enigmatic. "Trust me."

Peter stepped forward. "Lucy, if you're in trouble, we can help. You don't have to face this alone."

But Lucy merely laughed, a sound that carried a hint of bitterness.

"Oh, Peter," she said, her voice tinged with sadness. "I'll be okay. I want only the best for both of you. Today is day one of the rest of my life."

With those words, she turned and walked back towards the ship, her figure growing smaller in the distance. Sarah and Peter watched her go, knowing that she meant it. They would never see her again.

Peter and Sarah now walked with linked arms. With a heavy sigh, Sarah climbed into the car. As Peter pulled away, she looked out the window, watching the world pass by in a blur of colours and shapes.

She knew that the road ahead would be long and complicated, that the ghosts of the past would continue to haunt them. But she also knew that they had each other and that together, they could face anything.

As the car sped away from the dock, Sarah closed her eyes, letting the rhythmic hum of the engine lull her into a sense of calm. Whatever the future held, she was ready to face it, one step at a time.

Peter reached over and took Sarah's hand, gently squeezing it.

"We're going to be okay," he said softly, his voice barely audible over the engine's rumble.

"We've got each other, and that's all that matters."

Sarah nodded; her eyes still closed. She knew he was right.

"I just can't shake this feeling," she murmured, her voice trembling slightly. "Like something terrible is about to happen."

Meanwhile, back onboard the Emerald Empress, Lucy walked through the empty lobby of the ship, knowing there was one conversation she still needed to have.

CHAPTER TWENTY-NINE

SIX MONTHS EARLIER

MARBLE ARCH HOTEL, LONDON

The dim light from the bedside lamp cast a warm glow over Lucy and Edward's entwined naked bodies. Their breaths mingled as they lay tangled in the hotel room's luxurious sheets.

They had rarely been able to spend the entire night together.

"Lucy, I've never felt this way about anyone before," Edward whispered, his voice low and soft.

She shifted even closer to him, feeling the heat of his body against her own, which provided her with a sense of security that had long been absent from her life.

"Edward, our love is something special, isn't it?" she murmured, her eyes searching his for reassurance. She did not want to hear his love for her; she wanted to know that her deception was working. She had him completely under her spell.

"My darling. You have no idea how much I want us to be together," he confessed, the vulnerability in his voice drawing her even closer.

"Would you do anything for me, Edward?" Lucy asked, her voice soft but laced with an undercurrent of determination. Knowing he was trapped.

"Anything, Lucy. You know that, and I'll prove it."

"Thank you. I love you," Lucy replied as she hugged him.

"Then run away with me, Lucy, when all this is done. Let's build a life together, away from all this," he implored, his eyes capturing hers with an intensity that took her breath away.

"Edward... I want that more than anything. But there's so much at stake. We must be careful, plan everything out, and stick to the plan with Graham, the cruise, and everything else. You know we'll have to stay apart for months after we return," she replied cautiously, maintaining her composure.

"Of course, Lucy. We'll take it one step at a time. But I promise you, we will have the future we both deserve," Edward vowed, his sincerity evident.

"Promise me, Edward. Promise me you'll never let anyone or anything come between us," Lucy suggested, her voice wavering as she was momentarily vulnerable, knowing she didn't intend anything.

"Lucy, I swear it. Nothing will ever come between us. You have my heart, and that bond can never be broken," he declared.

As he held her close, Lucy found solace in the strength of his embrace, allowing herself to believe, if only for a moment, that their love was genuine, although it never had been.

Lucy smoothed the creases of her silk blouse, her fingers trembling ever so slightly. Still lying in bed, Edward watched as Lucy started to get dressed. She had to remain calm and collected. She could not let Edward see through her carefully crafted game.

"Edward," she began, her voice steady despite the turmoil.

"What I said before, I need you to understand that our relationship has to stay a secret. If anyone were to find out, it would destroy everything we're trying to build together. Imagine if suspicion fell on us after, you know…"

"Of course, Lucy," he replied without hesitation, his eyes filled with concern.

"I would never do anything to jeopardise what we have."

"Thank you," she said, allowing herself a small smile. Inside, she marvelled at how easily she could manipulate him. He was completely enamoured with her, and for now, that worked in her favour.

"So, I want to ask outright, you'll help him to fall off the boat?" Lucy looked directly at Edward.

"Of course, and I understand, any acknowledgement that we were together before Graham's slip would raise suspicion," said Edward, looking around the room as if worried someone could be listening to their conversation.

"So, we stick to the plan. I arrange for my group to be on the Emerald Empress. On night one, Graham goes overboard, and the ship turns around; there's also a part two, but I'll get to that. I don't want to spend any longer than I have to with those people, so we wait six months before getting together so it doesn't look odd. Completely believable, you comfort a grieving widow, and we fall in love."

"Perfect," said Edward, looking pleased with himself.

"Sometimes I think I should just leave him, but I would never be free, never be completely free. He would never let me go. He's more controlling than anyone sees." Lucy looked down.

"Things will work out, and it's our secret. We also need the money."

"Our secret," said Lucy.

"Speaking of secrets, where is Graham now?" Edward asked, his curiosity piqued.

"He doesn't suspect anything?"

"Every Tuesday and Thursday, I tell him I'm attending Pilates classes," Lucy explained, her tone matter-of-fact.

"In reality, I'm here with you. As far as he knows, I'm just trying to stay fit and healthy."

"Lucy, you're brilliant, and you do look very fit and healthy," Edward remarked, his admiration genuine, but comments like that made Lucy's skin crawl.

"Edward, this may sound paranoid, but I can't shake the feeling that someone might be watching us," Lucy confessed, her eyes darting around the luxurious suite.

"We need to be extra cautious."

"Lucy, my dear, I promise I'll do everything in my power to protect you," Edward vowed, his hand brushing against her cheek with a tenderness that made her shiver.

"Thank you," she murmured, leaning into his touch momentarily before pulling away.

Lucy lay back down on the bed, half-dressed, just wearing a blouse, not entirely happy with the lack of detail in their conversation. Opportunities to talk before putting things in place would be scarce.

The flickering candlelight cast eerie shadows on the hotel room's walls, looking like characters in a prophecy of what would come. She knew she had to convince Edward that their plan was fool proof or risk losing everything they had worked so hard to achieve.

"Edward, we mustn't forget that our ultimate goal is freedom–not just for ourselves, but also from Graham," Lucy said, her voice barely above a whisper.

"We've been meticulous in planning this, and suspicion must fall on Denny. So, I've got an idea. Graham falls overboard, then the next night, we get Denny drunk, get his phone, he goes overboard, and we send a message from his phone to his wife Terri confessing that he pushed Graham off."

"But why involve Denny?" Edward looked confused. "We can just say Graham slipped; it's much easier."

"Denny is a monster, Edward; it's a convenient way to tie everything up; they hate each other; it's completely believable." Lucy could tell that Edward hated the plan.

"If you loved me, Edward, you would trust me on this." she knew he would do anything.

"Of course, my love," Edward agreed, "But how do we ensure that happens?"

"Leave that to me," Lucy replied, her expression unreadable.

"On the first night of the cruise, I'll arrange for Graham and Denny to have a heated argument in front of witnesses. It won't be difficult–their hatred is well-known, and Denny's temper is notorious."

"Very clever," Edward mused, clearly impressed by her cunning.

"So, once there's a motive, all we need to do is make sure Graham slips over the railing, and that's for me."

"Exactly," she affirmed, her eyes cold and calculating.

"With you controlling security, we can orchestrate the perfect alibi. I even thought I might invite them all around for a meal before we go, get the rivalry simmering."

Lucy couldn't afford any mistakes, not when the stakes were this high, but she knew it was all she would think about for the next six months. As she glanced at Edward, she saw the trust in his eyes and felt a pang of guilt. She couldn't let him know that her true intentions differed from his. Not yet, anyway. She was using him.

"Lucy," Edward murmured, taking her hand in his, "I want you to know that I'm with you every step of the way. Together, we'll rid ourselves of Graham and Denny and finally be free to live the life we deserve."

"Thank you, Edward," she replied.

"I couldn't do this without you. I want to be yours."

"Edward… there's something you need to know about Denny," Lucy began, her voice barely audible yet laden with emotion.

"He didn't only hurt me–he destroyed the life of my friend, Sarah."

Edward's grip tightened around Lucy, his eyes narrowing as he listened intently.

"What happened?"

"Years ago, when I was first married to Graham, Denny came into our lives in a way he hadn't before," she explained, her voice quivering with anger.

"He seduced Sarah, promising her the world. But then he abandoned her and used her, leaving her heartbroken and destitute. I won't explain, but he's an evil guy."

"Lucy, I'm so sorry," Edward murmured, his thumb gently stroking her cheek.

"Sarah couldn't bear the pain and humiliation," Lucy continued, tears glistening.

"Lucy…" Edward breathed, his expression a mixture of anguish and rage.

"That monster must pay for what he's done to both of you."

"Exactly," she replied, her voice regaining its steeliness.

"That's why framing him for Graham's murder is so important to me. It's not just about freedom from my husband; it's about avenging the friend I have. Sarah is so important to me."

"Consider it done," Edward said, his voice unwavering as he held her closer.

"Thank you," she whispered, her eyes meeting his.

Lucy lay in Edward's arms, tricking herself into thinking she was safe. She could feel his breath on her neck, the rise and fall of his chest as he slept soundly beside her. In the calm darkness, Lucy turned to face him, studying the lines that time had etched upon his face.

“Edward,” she whispered, testing the waters of the quiet night. He stirred but did not wake. Lucy knew she was using him, but knew it was necessary collateral damage to her master plan.

CHAPTER THIRTY

WEDNESDAY NIGHT 8.30 PM

THE EMERALD EMPRESS

DAY FIVE OF THE CRUISE

Lucy stood outside Edward's suite.

This was the most difficult of all the things she had done so far. She had promised him her whole world only to make Edward do what he'd done, to help her in the way she needed. Their affair had only lasted for the last eight months, but Lucy knew this was necessary to get Edward over the line to commit the most unimaginable crime. Money wouldn't have been enough; Lucy knew he needed to do it for love. She walked into Edward's suite, closing the door behind her. Edward looked up from his desk, his face lighting up with joy at the sight of her.

"Finally, we're here, where we've both always wanted to be. The plan didn't exactly go to plan, but we got it done." He stood and opened his arms wide.

"Edward," Lucy whispered with a slight shake of her head.

"I'm not here to tell you what you want to hear." Edward's face completely changed in an instant.

His worst nightmares were coming true. Since the start of all of this, this was his most significant risk, and he didn't know if things would pay off until he committed his crime.

He was in love, and that had driven him. Lucy stopped short, keeping her distance. Her eyes were cold as she looked at him.

"Don't."

"Don't what? But Lucy, we can finally be together, as planned. These past five years…"

"Stop," Lucy's voice was sharp, "just stop."

Edward faltered, confused by her demeanour. This wasn't the heartfelt reunion he had envisioned. His world was about to crumble, and he knew it.

"Lucy, what is it? Tell me." He took a step toward her.

"I know this has all been tough. It's been a tough few days. Just take your time."

She backed away, shaking her head.

"No, Edward. Things have changed."

He searched her face, trying to understand. This couldn't be happening, not after everything.

"I love you, Lucy. You know that. I know you love me too...this is a lot to take in." Edward was now shaking.

"Love?" Lucy scoffed, her voice dripping with disdain.

"You thought I loved you? I was using you, Edward. All this time, it was just a means to an end. Do I feel bad about it? No. You're just one of them, and now I'm free of you all. I heard all the stories about you and other women. I was just another of those. You use people all the time; think about the carnage you've left behind."

Edward's face crumpled, his eyes searching hers for any sign of the warmth he once knew.

"No, you weren't. You never were. We had something special, Lucy. We had plans... I did everything for you, for us. I killed for you. This is all ours now."

Lucy's lips curled into a cruel smile.

"Plans? My only plan was to start a new life far away from you and everything else. And now, I'm going to do just that."

Desperation clawed at Edward's heart. Lucy felt she might be going in a bit tough, but she knew that was best; she couldn't leave him with any hope.

But for him, this couldn't be happening. He needed her now more than ever.

"Lucy, please. You can't leave me. Not now. The business... the ships... I need your help. I love you."

She laughed, a cold, mirthless sound.

"Your business? Why should I care about your failing little cruise ship? I have what I need from you, Edward. There's nothing left for me here. I don't want to see you again."

Edward reached for her, his hands trembling.

"But we can fix it together. Just give me a chance. I know you'll change your mind if you --"

"Enough!" Lucy snapped, her composure cracking for a moment. She took a deep breath, smoothing her features into an icy mask.

"I won't be changing my mind, Edward. It's over. I'm leaving, and you can do nothing to stop me. Now you know how it feels to be used."

She turned on her heel, ready to leave his life forever.

"No, Lucy, don't do this", Edward shouted after her.

"You can't. You're all I have." He had now slumped to his knees, a broken man on all fours crying into the ground.

With a final glance over her shoulder, Lucy's heart twinged with pity for the man she was leaving behind. But she had decided, and there was no turning back now. She took a deep breath and firmly settled on the path ahead.

She gracefully glided back through the opulent lobby and gathered her lone suitcase, filled only with the bare necessities needed for a fresh start. The rest of her belongings would remain aboard the ship with the memories of the last few days, a reminder of the life she was leaving behind. She could feel the weight of opportunity and adventure resting on her shoulders as she headed towards her new beginning.

Lucy strode through the bustling crowd of passengers disembarking the ship, the smell of the port, oil, and water. Her head was held high, and her heart raced with relief and anticipation. The curious glances from those around her barely registered. She was finally free—free of everyone. It was her against the world.

Freedom.

No more suffocating expectations, no more pretending to be someone she wasn't. This was her chance to start fresh, to build a life on her terms.

She hadn't even decided which way to turn out of the car park at the dock. She didn't know what she was going to do next. Their car had been driven to the pier by Graham. She wasn't even sure where it was parked. She may return home; she may not. For someone who had meticulously planned every step of the last days, she hadn't planned for this, but that's how she wanted it from now on.

As she walked, Lucy's mind drifted back to Edward, broken and pleading on the floor of his suite. A twinge of guilt pricked at her conscience, and she wondered if she might return and ensure he was ok. She knew it would have been kinder to have had a discussion, maybe taking a few hours over it, to have kept in contact at least, but she knew this way was the only way to do it. It would be challenging, but he needed to get over it. She couldn't afford to let sentimentality cloud her judgment, not when she was so close to achieving her future, the one she had dreamed of for years.

She stood in a large open square next to the ship, with high buildings and multi-storey car parks for the port. The Emerald Empress, which made up the fourth side of the square, was still illuminated. Around her, the crowd began to disperse. Each person was caught up in their own life and destinations. Lucy blended in seamlessly, just another face in the sea of lost souls. She smiled, relishing the anonymity of being just another stranger; no one here knew her, and she liked that. Suddenly, Lucy felt compelled to look back at the ship as if someone were watching her. There he was, the silhouette of Edward, standing alone in the same place the group had seen him when they arrived on his private deck, way up high. She couldn't see his face, but his stance conveyed a broken man.

Without thinking, she raised her hand and waved, making a final farewell gesture. Not a happy wave, but a wave to say goodbye. She watched as Edward's shoulders slumped, his body sagging under the weight of his grief. His turmoil was evident, a silent plea for her to reconsider and return to him.

But Lucy's resolve remained unshaken. She had made her choice, and there was no turning back now. The consequences of her actions were his to bear, not hers.

Time seemed to slow down as Lucy witnessed Edward reaching into his pocket, his movements deliberate and purposeful. Her heart skipped a beat as she realised what he was about to do.

Edward was holding the same gun he had used earlier. He pulled the bullet magazine out, looked at it, and pushed it back in.

He raised it to his head, now standing entirely straight as if standing to attention.

Lucy felt a mix of shock and detachment wash over her, her mind struggling to process the scene unfolding before her eyes. She knew it wasn't worth shouting, not worth doing anything. The events would have to play out on their own.

Yet even as she watched, Lucy couldn't help but feel a flicker of pity for the man she had once called her lover. The importance of possibly witnessing the last moments of his life. He had been a pawn in her game, but she had never intended for it to come to this.

The seconds ticked by, each feeling like an eternity as Lucy waited for the inevitable.

A loud gunshot pierced the air, spreading panic and confusion among the disembarking passengers, who ran in every direction. Screams echoed through the square as people scattered, seeking shelter from the unseen danger. In the middle of everything, Lucy stood still.

She turned away as Edward's dead body slumped below view. She closed her eyes and walked through the panicked crowd. She knew there would be sacrifices, and there was no remorse.

As she disappeared, Lucy knew that she would never look back from that day on.

The silent wave of relief washed over her, and every step she took was a step toward her new life, a step toward her future.

THE END

Printed in Great Britain
by Amazon

54747272R00202